TO SWALLOW THE EARTH

To Swallow the Earth

the Earth

Ransom Wilcox
&
Karl Beckstrand

Premio Publishing
Midvale, UT, USA
PremioPublishing.com

To Swallow the Earth

by Ransom Wilcox & Karl Beckstrand

FIRST PREMIO PUBLISHING EDITION, MAY 2015
Copyright © 2015.
Midvale, UT, USA
A Barn Full o' Proud first PREMIO PUBLISHING & GOZO BOOKS edition,
2013 (under the title: *Horse & Dog Adventures in Early California*)

Published in the United States of America.

Also an ebook and audio book (soon to be a graphic novel). Order this and other multicultural adventures/ebooks via major distributors, booksellers, libraries, or PremioPublishing.com. For FREE online books, see PremioBooks.com.

Library of Congress catalog number: 2015937400
ebook ISBN: 978-1311882387 ISBN: 978-0692407974

31088100883444

For David, Jean, Debbie, and Barry

Before Reno—before the riches of Las Vegas—there was Carson City and the surrounding outposts that serviced the gold and silver mines that sprang up in Nevada's silver rush of the latter 1800s. The Comstock Lode and Ophir Mine brought people of all kinds to the territory—soon after called the Silver State. This land was rugged, as were the people.

TO SWALLOW
THE EARTH

I. Drop

With uplifted blacksnake, the stage driver pulled up the horses in front of Carson City's St. Charles Hotel. Patricia Laughlin stepped down. But the driver wasn't unloading her trunk and valises. Foot on the brake, he stared at a big man in a Stetson who had exploded from the Lake Saloon across the street, hands poised over a bone-handled gun at his hip. Patricia didn't notice the easy conceit of the big man's bearing; his focus forced her gaze to a man at her left, who had just untied a horse from the hitchrack.

Beneath the brim of a battered hat was a gaunt face and a nose that was slightly askew. He seemed unaware of the large-chested man in the Stetson, the contempt that smoldered above his unlit cigar (spittle dark from much chewing and little smoking). As the gaunt man led his horse in a half turn, his mount was interrupted from the front of the saloon.

"Forester!"

Patricia now saw dark eyes and jet black hair under the battered hat and a shirt that was streaked with soot smudges, as though he had just ridden through a burned-over area. The Colt that sagged at his hip was well used, and the cartridge belt held only a handful of shells. The dark eyes disappeared again as the man turned toward the cigar under the Stetson.

The big man stepped deliberately to the street as all other feet stilled. Subconsciously, the girl read the faces within the range of her vision. On one, she saw a self-satisfied smirk. On others, she caught a look of half-hidden fear. Others were expressionless, as though their owners wished to be neutral; most were attuned to the prospect of witnessing violence.

Unfettered tongues had prophesied this moment, built up its importance until it seemed inevitable. Now Bridger Calhoun and Wade Forester were finally going to have it out. Bridger's voice boomed the length of the street. "You've been saying things behind my back, Forester."

"Only because you weren't around for me to say them to your face," said Forester, untwisting a rein.

"I'm here."

"I see you."

"Then play your hand."

"I won't pull on you," said Wade. "If I wanted that, I'd have found you long before this."

"You—"

"Think what you like."

"I'm thinkin' it."

"Your privilege." Wade put his hands on the saddle.

Bridger moved forward again, his legs bent slightly. His eyes shimmied with a lethal desire straining to explode.

Wade turned from the horse. Spectator eyes followed his right hand. It moved from the saddle to the buckle of his gun belt. A quick tug and the belt dropped to the dust.

The only sound now was a paper handbill fluttering in the

breeze; if it had known the disgrace that had just occurred, it would have held its peace. This was something the people would long remember.

Forester picked up the gun belt, buckled and draped it on the saddle horn, then mounted his horse. From his perch, he saw Bridger's arrogant face go blank. He reined his horse slowly about and rode south, out of town.

The people stirred slowly—as if loath to accept what had happened. Bridger Calhoun was not a professional gunman in the strictest sense. He was well known. He had called his man out. Wade Forester had refused the challenge, refused to come to tow in a public meeting; now he could not but be branded a coward.

Bridger turned from watching the back of his foe and caught sight of the young woman on the hotel porch. Her eyes were fixed on the smudged stranger disappearing in the distance. Bridger doffed his hat and approached her with a welcoming smile.

"Am I addressing Miss Patricia Laughlin?"

"Yes. You must be Mr. Calhoun. My father has written to me about you many times." The dark-haired woman extended a gauntleted hand, "I'm happy to make your acquaintance. Is my father in town to meet me?"

"Miss Laughlin, I am sorry to report that he was unable to come at this particular time. He's been feeling poorly. Last week, he went to Virginia City on business and ended up stuck there under doctor's care. Now don't be alarmed; they just didn't want him traveling too soon. He wired and asked me to do the honor of escorting you down to the ranch. He said he'd meet us there in a day or so."

"Is it serious?"

"I don't think so. You know how your father burns the candle, so to speak." Patricia nodded sullenly. "I must apologize for the incident you just witnessed," said Bridger. "Had I known you were already here, I assure you, this embarrassment would not have occurred. Believe me, I'm deeply sorry."

"Who was that man? What was the trouble?"

"Let's just say he's a nobody who got a little out of line. How was your trip? No trouble from Black Bart, I hope."

Patricia's eyebrows rose. "The Gentleman Bandit must have had other appointments this week."

Bridger smiled. "I have a spring wagon over here. I can load your trunk and baggage, and we can be on our way."

"I'm just a little tired from the trip." Patricia looked up at the hotel sign. "Couldn't we leave tomorrow?"

"If you wish. However, it's quite a distance. If we can do twelve miles today, we can stay overnight at Genoa and then get an early start in the morning."

"I guess I can stand another twelve miles. Would you give me a spell to freshen up a little?"

"Surely. I'll call for you. Is there anything you need in the meantime, anything at all I can get you?"

"No, I don't think so. Thanks very much."

II. Assessment

Bridger Calhoun pulled the team up for a short blow as the dust they had been stirring overcame the wagon. Little rivulets of sweat darkened the coats of the dappled grays and the skin over their withers twitched.

During the ride, Bridger had cast a few surreptitious glances at the girl in her corduroy skirt and waistcoat. Each had had an opportunity to size the other up.

"Would you like some water?" asked Bridger.

"No, thank you," said Patricia. "I may at the next stop. My father says you've managed lots of spreads."

"Well, mostly I've been hired by prospectors to help them stake their claims. I've seen fortunes come and go like dust devils, from California to Montana."

"I imagine some people handled that better than others."

"Oh, I'm not sure anyone easily endures a mine petering out or a jumped claim, for that matter. It's kind of an infection—avarice. I doubt there's a person alive that's immune." Bridger stole another glance, and Patricia gave him a mischievous smile from under her flat-crowned hat.

"Like what you see?" she asked.

Bridger grinned without self-consciousness. "I'd say you're a looker in any man's book." He lifted his chin. "What's the tally on your end?"

"Oh, I'd say you were handsome, aggressive, and you've had an education. Of course women are attracted to you, and you're spoiled rotten on that score."

"Guilty, I suppose. You're not completely unconscious of your own charms, but that would be a completely superfluous statement about any pretty girl."

"So?"

"So, we may as well get acquainted. Do you expect to stay out here?"

"I don't see why not." Patricia took off her gloves. "It's time I got to know my father. He sent me to San Francisco for finishing school years ago, after my mother left us. We were living in Sacramento at the time." Bridger looked at his boots, and Patricia realized she had better get back to small talk. "I've only been through this territory once."

"It was first settled by the Mormons," said Bridger, grateful to change the subject. "They built an outpost at Genoa before Carson was ever a city—or anything else. Of course, the Washoe people have been in the area for quite a while before any whites came. Then silver was found—I'm sure you know about that, since it brought your father and so many others here. It's still rough country, few conveniences and some tough characters who'll slit your throat for the price of a drink."

"Trying to scare me?"

"No, just preparing you. This isn't Frisco, with a policeman at your call in time of trouble."

"Like that trouble you were in back there?"

"Maybe."

"You seemed right noncommittal about that little affair. What's behind it, if you don't mind saying?"

"I guess you may as well hear it from me first. You're bound to get several garbled-up versions from gossipy tongues.

"A few years ago, I married a woman named Julia Forester, the daughter of Silas Forester, owner of the K-bar spread. We were going to have a child, but as the pregnancy progressed, she became mentally unbalanced. When she lost the baby, she completely lost herself—no memories—just incoherent groans. Nothing I did helped. She's back there in Carson now, a face without a heart or mind."

"I'm terribly sorry."

"Then Old Man Forester disappeared without a trace. The whole thing is a mess. The ranch was heavily mortgaged and losing a lot of stock to rustlers. I've kept it out of the bank's hands by making payments on the loans. If the old man is ever declared legally dead, I can, with Julia's share, claim title to the property.

"Now her brother, Wade, shows up with blood in his eye. He left here because he couldn't get along with the old man. He's been a vagabond, but now swears to get me because of some gossip he heard about me abusing Julia, causing her illness."

Patricia nodded again.

"So there it is. I confronted him to bring this thing out in the open. You saw how he crawled."

"After an episode like that, I doubt he'll have the courage to stay in the country."

"Oh, he'll be around stirring up trouble, I guarantee it."

Bridger picked up the lines, clucked to the team, and they proceeded at a trot. Over the grind of the wheels in the gravel and the clomping of the horses' hooves, Patricia managed to continue the conversation.

"You said my father wasn't well. How long? He didn't mention anything in his letters."

"I suppose he just didn't want to bother you. He's been working so hard and worrying. His plans depend on whether or not I can get clear title to the K-bar. Your uncle's done most of the spade work down in Blossom Valley. He's secured options on most of the land there—been working on it for the last two years. He's done a good job, believe me. I've worked with him and I have every respect for his ability."

"Sounds like something big."

"It's an empire. You should be proud. Someday, much of this area will belong to you."

"Just what is your role in this kingdom?"

"I have a sizable interest, a holding that will amount to nearly a third of it all. I've sort of been a trouble-shooter, the guy who handles the tough element—the rustlers, the hardheads, any bumps in the road."

Patricia surveyed the scenery ahead. "Will we get to the ranch tomorrow?"

"We'll make Gardnerville tomorrow. The ranch is about ten miles beyond. I think you'd better plan to stay in town until your father gets back from Virginia City. The ranch isn't exactly furnished for a lady, and the crew's a pretty rough bunch."

"I won't exactly be an Easter lily with all this grime I'm collecting."

"All the same, the Kent Hotel will have everything you need."

Patricia was so tired; letting the hotel tend her sounded about perfect.

III. Hungry

Wade Forester was hungry as only a trail-starved man can be after a day's fast. Blue dusk touched the sage and the pinion pines. Wade looked on the green patch of a pond. He had been on this spot for an hour; the patience of an Indian scout held him to his task. Slowly, the .30-caliber Winchester came to his shoulder. A deer had walked warily into the clearing with uplifted head and sensitive ears keening the wind. It sensed an intruder, whirled, and sprang for cover in one swift, fluid motion. A slug caught it in the neck in midair, and it thrashed out its life on the ground.

Anticipating tender venison fillets, Wade cleaned the animal, rolled the hams in the hide, tossed them over his shoulder, and headed for his camp. He stopped to analyze a half-heard sound that came to him dimly on the wind, like a cry of distress, but he wasn't sure. The smell of wood smoke increased his puzzlement.

Topping a ridge in the dim twilight, he looked down on his campsite. His possibles were scattered, and the horse he had carefully staked out was gone. He circled the spot warily, keeping in the brush as much as possible. A pack rat scurried for cover, and a quail exploded from a pinion almost at his head.

Entering the campsite, he found a shambles of strewn flour, ripped blankets, and a saddle with the leather slashed beyond repair. In the half dark, he almost stumbled over his bay gelding. Risking the flare of a match, he whipped it to life and examined the horse. It had been stabbed repeatedly in the hindquarters, and its throat had been cut. The ground around it was cut and gouged by flailing hooves in the agonies of death.

This wanton killing was a warning and a threat. He was not wanted in this country—and he knew several good reasons why. He had been gone for three years. He had been sent to school in San Francisco, but quickly tired of reading about dead philosophers and dead civilizations. In a moment of bored rebellion, he shipped out on a freighter. What notion enters a kid's head that he has to get out and see what makes the wolf howl?

When the ship finally docked in New York, he learned of trouble at home via a letter from Dr. Charles Alexander, an old family friend. Once back in Carson, he had looked the good man up.

That experience was something he found hard to even think about. Dr. Alexander had taken Wade's sister, Julia, into his home and made sure her every need was conscientiously addressed. There she sat, a girl he had been more than a big brother to after their mother had died in childbirth. They had shared pranks, picnics, and adventures—real and imaginary. Julia was always willing to help anyone in need.

Now there was no word of greeting, no sign that she even knew who he was. Her heretofore sunny face was as expressionless as a display window dummy's. She was without sense or memory. Wade's frustration and grief combined to make him almost crazy. He had a wild desire to smash, to destroy whatever foul thing had gripped his sister and taken her from him.

Worst of all, Wade couldn't find his father. He had swallowed his pride, hoping the two of them could bring Julia back. But no one had heard from the man since he'd taken up prospecting for gold in the back country a year or so prior.

Later, Wade pieced out the story on Julia and, in a moment of rage, threatened to get the man who was responsible. But was any person responsible? Julia had been such a thoroughly healthy person. The doctor had pointed out that pregnancy, shock, or any number of things can throw the mind off balance.

But the word had gone out that Wade had threatened a brother-in-law he had never met. He hadn't meant to make accusations, but his rage and grief had been so great that he had spoken out of turn.

Now he thought on the episode in Carson City. For the first time in his life, he had been made to eat crow. Of course, he could have stood up like a man and drawn his gun, but some force stayed his hand. He was not sure of any person's guilt, and there was a vague warning bell deep within him that seemed to tell him to feel his way—slowly.

Now he was sure that something more than a single mortal enemy threatened his survival. He was unhorsed and alone, not knowing what men or group opposed him.

Since his return, he had heard of shady interests in the territory. A Pat Laughlin was buying up land in Blossom Valley until few privately owned acres remained. Terror seemed to be the main instrument for procuring titles to various small ranches. With no blood family to welcome him, even his mother territory seemed gravely against him.

He shook himself, hunched his shoulders into his mackinaw jacket, and considered his next move. There wasn't much of his camp gear to salvage. He slung the meat to his shoulders again and took off southward in hopes of finding someone who would lend him a horse and saddle.

It was dark except for a mere crescent of a moon. As he slogged along the trail, he was tempted to rid himself of the venison that weighed on his thin frame. The trail turned down a ridge and passed through a dense clump of sage.

Clearing the sage, he heard a rustle and a footfall in the distance to his right. Before he could turn, two flaming streaks lanced out at him in the darkness. He plunged forward and laid still, the reverberations of the shots rolling over him.

A voice called to another out of the darkness. "We got the sucker dead center. I heard them thirties hit like they was going into a gut-shot doe. May as well see if it's the hombre the boss wanted. He sure came from the right direction—and the wrong trail, for him."

"Suppose it ain't the right feller?"

"His tough luck for being out here."

Two figures materialized out of the dark blob of sagebrush. As they approached the prostrate form, they were voluble in bragging about their straight shooting skills, in the dark, at long range. When they were within eight feet of Wade's prone figure, he suddenly came to life like a striking rattler. Light blossomed from Wade's guns. The reports went rolling across the sagebrush as the acrid odor of burnt powder hung in the air.

Both men went down, the taller one with a horrible scream rattling from his throat. Wade rolled away from the venison and held a ready pistol on the two. Moving closer, he cautiously prodded one with a boot toe. He was dead. Squatting by the second man, Wade looked for signs of life, but found none. This was somewhat of a disappointment because he would like to have asked a few pertinent questions.

After a little scouting, Wade found two horses. He stripped

the gear from one and turned it loose. Mounted on the other, he felt whole again. He rode all night, angling out of the desert to the higher country to the west.

The sage grew higher and the pinion pines more profuse. Wade was emerging from a little copse of tamarack as daylight broke. Suddenly, over a shallow ridge came the baying of hounds. Two tan and white dogs, ears flapping wildly, came loping down the trail. Wade's horse danced and shied as the dogs snapped at its muzzle, blooping and baying as though they had treed a grizzly. A shrill whistle floated out on the morning air.

IV. News

A scarecrow caricature of a man appeared. He rode a dun-colored pony with short hind legs, a huge chest, and narrow hips that gave it a high-in-front, buffalo effect. When he saw Wade, the rider flipped a long leg over the saddle horn and hit the ground in a mad forward charge. Wade leaped to the ground and met this man with a terrific impact that landed them both in the brush clawing, struggling, and cursing with uncomplimentary language. The dogs closed in, snapping and howling.

Finally the scuffle subsided and the two sat up, blowing and red-faced from the exertion. Each had a grin that threatened to split his face.

The tall man had a long, protruding chin that earned him the nickname—behind his back—of Hatchet-Face Milo. He was a government trapper who spent his time shooting or trapping predators. He had few friends, but Wade was the best of the select few.

His voice was a booming, gratey bass that could carry across a canyon. He said, in his quietest manner, which made the manzanita leaves vibrate, "Where ya been you ol' slab o' seajerky? Man, you's a sight for sore eyes, even if you's homelier'n a fin-horned toad."

"So I ain't pretty like you." Wade rubbed the ears of one of the sprawling hounds.

"Say, that's how come I quit shaving so often. Got so's I couldn't stand the sight of my own face. It's God's own mercy I can push this mess around in front of me without having to look at it myself. Course with all my smarts, I don't need good looks."

"How long does it take your Adam's apple to traverse that turkey neck?"

"Never mind the flattery. You's up here for something besides palaverin' about me. You want a breakdown of happenings, no?"

"I thought you'd be as good a one to see as any."

Milo scuffed at the soil with a worn, run-over boot heel and squirted an accurate charge of tobacco juice that upended a wandering beetle.

"Your pa disappeared a couple a summers back," he said with sudden somberness. "I tried to cut his trail, but pffft, no luck. Once he was out of the way, somebody jumped the Jason mine. Of course, the K-bar's bein' run by Julia's husband. We's had two rotten years. Not only has the ore petered out, most of the cattle is gone, and the small ranchers have been sold out or scared out. Them's as stayed was hit by a passel of fires and such. Some night-lead flew around—careless like, if you know what I mean—ended up under some people's skin. Mighty discouragin' to lose your barn, your house, or your skin that way."

Wade held his soot-smudged shirt out from his chest. "I've

seen the pattern. Found Chet Southworth dead behind his burned out ranch house. Who's behind it?"

"Dunno for sure. They's some wompin' big doin's goin' on. Scum and saddle tramps is gettin' big wages. Whole sections of land is bein' took over—some big operation with big plans."

"How did they get hold of the K-bar?"

"Ain't you heard what's happened to Julia?" Wade could only nod. "I found her heading on foot toward Alkali Lake—didn't even know me. I brought her to Doc Alexander's, but—"

"I've seen her," Wade broke in. "She was in no condition to tell me anything. She just sits there and stares at nothing."

Milo's long face grew longer. "Wade, if I was sure who'd done it, I'd get him out in the middle of a salt flat and turn my dogs on him. I'm dang near sure; but a body cain't go mixin' into somebody else's private affairs without no proof. Julia married this Bridger Calhoun. Bein' her husband, he's got some rights, 'specially with you gone. She went off of her . . . Heck! He's been runnin' the ranch with no one to tell him otherwise."

"There's a deed of transfer made out to a Pat Laughlin in Carson. I doubt if it's legal." It was more of a question from Wade.

"See, this Laughlin's a mystery to most folks," said Milo. "Hard to fight a body you never see. And, legal or not, it'd be a heck of a fight for you to get any say-so about the ranch. Your pa didn't leave no will, and since you waren't 'round, it's Julia's spread . . . well, leastwise till you turned up. Calhoun's been some sort of trustee of her share. Was her name on the deed?"

"It looked like her signature."

"As I say, it's all mixed up, and unwindin' 'er is liable to be migh-ty tricky."

"Any way you look at it, half of the ranch is mine."

"Sure, sure. And what good is a range without cows? They's a few head of horses, like the one you're riding, wearing your brand. You just sashay down there and move in on the ranch and see what happens. There'd be buzzard shadders flittin' over your carcass in less than forty-eight hours. Word being around that you's in the country, you don't need to claim the ranch or the mine to get yourself killed. Just stand still long enough for them bounty hunters to get you in their sights."

"It's been tried."

"Ain't surprised none." Milo spat again. "Now Wade, don't be seven kinds of a fool. Shuck outta here while your skin don't leak. You's young. No sense at all in gettin' yourself killed. They's other ranges and places to get another start."

"You know better than to give me that kind of advice."

"Yeah, dang it, I know. All a same, don't try 'er alone. You got some friends left. Get help afore you tackle it."

"Pull you into something that isn't your affair?"

"Heck, boy, she's my affair whether you want her that way or not! Your pa and me was real close. Besides, all your old friends is already in it. Them as could help you the most is bein' rawhided to get them out of the territory. They got to fight or go under."

"I tangled with Calhoun in Carson."

"Heard about that already." Milo put his head down. "Bad news travels fast."

"I couldn't pull on him. Julia might be in love with him. Heck of a note if I killed her husband."

"Heard he made you crawl."

"He sure did."

"He probably don't know how lucky he was you backed down."

"I'm praying Julia gets her senses back. One word from her, and he's bought and paid for. What kind of a character is this guy?"

"Brother Bob, there is a migh-ty cool one. He hits this country just after you left, sweet talkin' as a Don Juan. He sweeps Julia off of 'er feet a couple of years back, and she ain't but just barely growed. No mistake, he's the front man for them big augers in this here section. He'll chin with you and give you that big smile, perlite as peaches, then he'll send some boys 'round to set fire to your hayfield. Soon he's dropped by lookin' sorrowful-like and offerin' to buy you out—as a favor to you! He'll take some watchin' and a sight of lickin' afore he backs down."

"What about the Jason mine?"

"Ain't been worked since your pa dis'peared. She's in the same boat as the K-bar as far as title is concerned."

Wade straightened. "I've got to go alone for a spell, until I get the lay of the land."

Milo rose to one knee. "I'll keep my eyes peeled. If I run onto anything, I'll find you some way. What you got wrapped in that there deer hide?"

Wade untied the bundle he'd been lugging around. Milo flipped the green hide away from the meat and stared in slack-jawed disbelief. With no effort to hide his sarcasm he boomed, "Where'd you learn t' shoot, Junior? Forget all I learned you about saggin' your belly, figurin' windage and light? It looks as how you was tryin' to grind the meat afore the deer quit kickin'."

He threw a rock in disgust. "I ain't never seen a more messed up pair of hams. You gettin' so's you can't hit the biggest part of a target?"

"Don't go yipping down the wrong trail, you old lizard-eater," said Wade, standing. "I broke that buck's neck at two hundred yards in bad light. Those slugs in there were meant for me. They won't shoot somebody in the back again."

"They? Two of 'em?"

"Yeah. And both riding K-bar horses. Looks like the word's out and the bounty hunt is on."

Wade swung up, headed up the trail, and waved to Milo, who had a doleful look on his face.

V. Interruption

Minden was a great metropolis of five buildings, three of which had recently been abandoned as silver mines started to peter out. The most prepossessing building was a red brick, two-story affair with eight-foot high windows closed in by rusty iron shutters. This hulk of a coffin seemed to hover over a little shanty at its side, which proclaimed itself a restaurant via a faded, almost illegible sign that said EAT.

Wade, riding out of the western high country, reined up before the shack and dismounted. He pulled back the screen door and exposed a greasy counter with five stools. A hinged section of the counter to the left of the door opened to the counter's rear.

A Chinese man came out and took Wade's order. In a few minutes, the usual fare of steak, bread, and cold beans was before him.

Wade's meal was nearly finished when the squeaky hinges of the screen door advertised the entrance of new arrivals at his left. He turned slowly to survey the two men who entered. One was a balding, phlegmatic man who was running to paunch. His glasses were so thick he could probably see into the future. The other was a scrawny kid of about nineteen or twenty. Red-yellow, unkempt hair matted his forehead under a greasy hat.

"It ain't Jobey," the kid said to his companion. His features were uneven. His mouth was a cruel line slathered with tobacco juice. He was the most dangerous kind: a reputation-hunting punk looking for personal glory and excitement. There was no cultural restraint here, no emotional control, only a twisted, beaten-down ego that knew only violence. He wore this demeanor like a badge of superiority.

Stabbing his eyes at Wade, he said with sarcastic poison, "Well, if it ain't the yellow-belly who backed down in Carson. Whatcha' doing ridin' a K-bar horse? You're in trouble, you saddle tramp. Last man on that horse was Jobey Coulter. Where is he?"

"Take it easy, boy," the yellow-haired kid's companion spat. "Don't stir things so quickly. We've got plenty of help if we want to take him."

"Who needs help with a blockhead like him? He's the hairpin the boss is after—and I got 'im. Drop your gun belt, Blockhead, and come over here."

Wade tossed a coin on the counter, laid his own hard stare on the stocky man, and then studied the kid without speaking. He thought of the last screaming agonies of a good gelding and wondered if either of these two were capable of such an act. While it could have been one of those dead ones he had left back on the trail, a Bowie knife at the kid's belt demanded acknowledgment.

"You wouldn't be handy with that knife would you?" he said with his voice low, struggling for self-control. "Especially on a good horse taught to trust humans?" Wade put up a reassuring hand. "I know, calling you human is stretching the point considerably."

The kid's yellow eyes dilated, and a smirk played on his features. "I seen it, mister. It sure was nice to watch your horse. My, but your feet must be sore."

There was no question that these bounty hunters were set to get Wade. Wade knew he was in an awkward position to try to get his gun out. He half turned to his food. Reaching for the salt shaker, his right hand continued in a sweeping arc, collecting the pepper, oil bottle, and sugar bowl too—all flew at the kid's head. The kid ducked. Wade flung himself over the counter.

The stocky man lurched out the door to safety. But the kid was not to be denied his play. He drew and thumbed a shot at Wade. Wade returned fire under the hinged section of the counter. The kid took it in the belly and pitched backward. He ripped the screen from its frame as he fell through the door. Wade moved out and bent over the kid, who lay on his back, moaning.

"Who stabbed my horse?"

"Go to hell, you stinking sheepherder."

Wade heard the pound of hooves before he turned and saw three riders sweep around the corner at a dead run. The stocky man waved a duo toward Wade. They rode at him with lead and flame spouting. Wade got one away before he made a jump for the doorway. But a horse struck him and smashed him hard against the wall of the shanty. His senses spun into oblivion.

***

Gardnerville would never be a ghost town. Even before the gold fever struck the country, it boasted three two-story buildings: the bank, the hotel, and Wilder's Mercantile. There were several frame buildings with porches and balconies, a church, a feed yard, stage depot, and express office. The road from the north was a mile-long avenue of poplars. There was the Kent House, now a hotel; a livery stable next to a pasture enclosed by a fence that ran down to, and along, the river; and the Fricke blacksmith shop, which faced the saloon. Near the north edge of town was Doc McFall's house, and beyond that was a burial plot that had achieved the dignity of being called a cemetery (rather than "Boot Hill").

Wade's senses pulsed back to him, bringing with them the pain of deep bruises. An effort to move his arm brought a stab of pain to his shoulder. He moved a hand slowly to his face, which felt numb, and found a nut-like swelling on his upper lip. One eye opened with considerable effort. He saw a huge freighter wheel suspended by a rope from the ceiling and supporting several dimly-lit kerosene lamps. He tried an experimental movement of a leg and was rewarded with a wrenching cramp in the calf. His whole body felt like it had been worked over with a lead riding quirt.

His head was clearing. He seemed to be lying against the back wall of a saloon. He could smell the pungent odors of whiskey, manure-covered boots, and the sour smell of unwashed bodies. He rotated his granite-like head. All he could see was an ant's-eye view of a forest of chair and table legs and a collection of boots in various stages of wear. The mumbled buzz brought fragments of information to him.

"Do we string the SOB up?"

"Naw, he's so bad stove-up he wouldn't know what was going on. Should've seen him bounce off that wall. Bet he lost half the skin on his face."

"Wonder if he's the jasper the boss wants."

"From what I hear tell, it's him; half-Mexican with no place to call home."

"It'd be funny if he was some innocent pilgrim. Hey, Slim, what happened in that restaurant anyways?"

Wade heard the answer of the paunchy man who had been in the little café with the kid. "That dang kid got a mite overanxious. Man, you should have heard him tell this character off. Bit off more than he could chew, though."

"Where was you at, Slim? How come you didn't side him?"

"'Cause I ain't no hero. That hairpin is plenty crazy. The kid made his fool play solo when there was four of us to handle it. Serves him right."

"How come he turned yeller back in Carson?"

"Ask him."

A general guffaw went up, then another voice became dominant. "Boy, that sister of his is sure a looker. Was you there when her and Bridger had that row over signin' them papers? Myself, I don't like my women so spunky."

"I warn't there, but Buzz, Curly, and I betch'a Gila Red was in on it. She fought like a catamount. Myself, personal, don't hold to treatin' no woman that-a-way, not even no digger squaw."

"Wonder if she'll ever get her marbles back."

Wade lay dormant, considering his chances. The sentence had been passed on him—that was certain. The killing of whoever had tried to bushwhack him on the trail, and now the kid, had sealed his doom. He tensed and relaxed his muscles to work some of the soreness and stiffness out. One thing he was sure of: it would be suicide for him to wait for his fate to take him. If he had any chance, it would have to be now while these men were off guard.

It took considerable effort to roll silently over on his stomach. He finally accomplished it at the expense of a lightening jab of pain through his temples. The deep hurt of his muscles almost brought a groan. He came slowly to his knees, his whole body quivering. He pushed against the wall and fought the nausea that gripped him; he was finally able to stand erect and look about. His movement began to dull the pain.

He was in Bondetti's Saloon, recognizing it from his many visits in his youth. Behind him were the stairs. Before him on the left were several men at the bar. More sat at a row of poker tables to his right. He edged slowly along the wall and finally reached the end of the bar. He waggled a finger at the bartender who set a glass of whiskey in front of him.

The bartender swiped at the bar top with a towel and absentmindedly glanced at his latest customer. He stared for a second, then said, "Hey! Ain't this the waddy that got run over by a horse?"

The turmoil, conversation, and horseplay were suddenly ruptured by a dead quiet. Every eye turned to the man at the end of the bar. Wade stood as nonchalantly as anyone, the glass of whiskey in his left hand. His clothes were ripped, and his face was battered and bruised. Though unarmed, he seemed more intent on finishing his drink than on any attempt to get away. The bartender and two men stood close by, but no one budged. Each waited for someone else to make a move.

Finally, the man next to Wade stepped back. He had curly brown hair and his upper lip was crisscrossed with three linear scars. Tentatively, he reached for his hip. He didn't have a chance to finish the draw. Wade's right elbow drove forward into his face, and the man dropped to his knees, blood gushing from his nose. As he fell, Wade snatched at his half-drawn gun with his right hand as his left hand pushed the hammer back hard.

There was a concerted movement toward Wade, who leaped to the top of the bar. Clutching hands tried to trip him. He kicked them aside or roweled them sharply with his spurs. In three running, dancing steps, he leaped for the freighter wheel that served as the makeshift chandelier.

He grabbed the rim, which tipped down. The opposite

edge smashed against the ceiling, and the lamps went out and cascaded on the men below. Wade's momentum swung him in an arc toward the batwing front doors. As he clung to the wheel, his feet churned and rose from the reaching hands that tried to snag him. Darkness brought a wild confusion of surging bodies. Wade let go and flew out the doors.

He hit the porch, lost his footing, and rolled down the two steps to end up under the tie rail. He rolled to his feet in a flash. Behind him there were curses, chairs and tables crashing, and some foghorn voice bellowing for light.

Any chance of escape would depend upon a good start—now. In seconds a body of men would be filling the air with lead and wrath. He ducked under the rail, jerked a Winchester from the scabbard on a horse, then reached over its back and shucked another one from the saddle. With one Winchester under his arm and the other held hip-high, he bounded back toward the doors just as two men charged out. He worked the lever, and orange lines of flame slashed at the oncoming men. They plunged backward to avoid this unexpected salutation. There was a maelstrom of movement as those rushing to get out stumbled over those seeking cover.

One Winchester ran dry. Wade flung it into the saloon. He dropped full-length under the doors and levered shot after shot into the seething mass of bodies. The hammer fell on an empty breech, and he left the rifle and leaped to the dirt.

In nearby buildings, wide-eyed faces appeared in windows and from behind door frames, but no one challenged Wade as he yanked two sets of reins from the tie rail, mounted one horse, and led another in a walk toward the edge of town. Again there was hesitation inside the saloon. Straining ears heard no pounding of hooves, no speedy exit.

Once out of town, Wade urged the horses into a gallop. In the middle of the long avenue of poplars, he heard the pursuit thundering after him. He put both horses to a run and held a steady pace. Another mile of this and he could see the hard-run horses getting closer. When he judged they were about four hundred yards in the rear, he changed horses and increased his speed until he was a half a mile in the lead.

At the top of a rise, he turned the lead horse loose and lashed him into a plunging run down the hill. He reined off to the side of the trail and waited. A mass of charging riders raced past him in pursuit of the riderless horse.

"Now what?" he thought. He looked back toward town. He reined his horse around and was soon back in Gardnerville.

He pictured how his unconscious ride from Minden must have been earlier that day. They had probably dangled him head down over a horse, like a butchered deer. Now his battered, weary body sagged in the saddle. He had to get some rest.

Gardnerville's streets were deserted. Wade approached the hotel from the rear, led his horse into a side alley, and dropped the reins so that anyone finding it would think it had simply strayed from the hitching rack.

Wade opened the rear door of the Kent Hotel and prospected the lobby before he entered. There was no one on duty as far as he could see. He spun the ledger around to see if there were any vacant rooms. A name jumped at him, knocking any plan he had out of his head. In neat, black script was written P. Laughlin.

Wade stood braced against the desk. White heat radiated through his pained frame, loosening his muscles. It was an ignition that surpassed fatigue. That name sparked a destructive madness. Ignoring the heightened ache in his head from his now pounding pulse, he turned on his heel. One burning pinpoint of action made him tiptoe up the stairs. He paused in front of the room registered to Laughlin. A crack of light showed under the door. He drew the borrowed pistol and checked the chambers.

Poised on one foot, he lifted the other, driving his heel against the door at the level of the lock. The door flew back against the wall with such force it almost leaped from the hinges. Wade stood in the doorway with gun stabbed before him. He was blinded by the sudden light and could not get his eyes to focus. When his eyes adjusted, he tried to make sense of the scene before him.

VI. Identity

A girl in a long, commodious nightdress stood in front of the mirror. A brush in her hand was frozen on her shiny dark hair, which rippled to her elbows. Shock and fear registered on her face.

Wade was immobile for a second, as was the girl. As he tipped the gun barrel down, Wade stammered, "Beg pardon, ma'am. This room is registered under the name of P. Laughlin."

The girl squinted, searching the face of this raw-boned intruder who looked as though he had been run over—and over again. Where there was still skin, three days' worth of stubble stuck out like iron filings on a magnet. One eye and a lip were grotesquely swollen. His tousled hair held bits of saloon sawdust matted by dried blood, and a bloody sleeve dangled in shreds from his shoulder. Though her mouth was dry, her rancor finally enabled her to spit out, "And suppose it is, does that give you any right to come barging into my room?"

"Excuse me. I only want to know where I can find Pat Laughlin."

The girl's quizzical look turned to recognition. With asperity, she said, "I'm Pat Laughlin."

"Pat?" Wade's voice was a hoarse croak. He straightened, as though the air had turned cold.

"Patricia Louise Laughlin. What's so shocking?" she asked in derision. "Is there any stigma attached to it?"

Wade's numbed senses fumbled to grasp the situation, but the murderous urge that had driven him to this room trumped his shock. Could this woman be the brains, the cipherer behind all that had happened to him?

"Is Bridger Calhoun your iron fist on the K-bar?"

The girl's chin rose. "In a way, yes."

"Takes your orders?"

Patricia was irked and defiant now. She said, "If I give him an order, he does it."

"His doings are under your orders."

"I've just said he bows to my wishes. Is it any business of yours, *Mister* Forester?"

"Maybe," he said measuredly. "Your waddies just missed killing me—more by accident than by intent. They're looking for me now to get it right. Now, maybe you don't know why they want me dead or maybe you're paying them to get rid of me. You may have impeccable reasons in your mind, so let's you and me have an understanding right now. If you want me dead, count on running the same gauntlet set up for me."*

Wade strode toward the girl. She stepped back, but he shoved her sideways to the bed with such force that she bounced and ended up on the floor in a sitting position.

Wade tore out one of her dresser drawers. "Have you a gun in this room?" She nodded dazedly. He dumped the filmy contents on the floor. Emptying another drawer, he found a .38 in an ornate holster attached to a belt. He pulled her to her feet, strapped the gun belt around her, and fastened the hefty buckle, somewhat askew. "There. You put yourself in a man's place, so by heaven you're going to get a man's treatment." Wade stepped back toward the door and stood, swaying a little. "Pull your gun!"

Patricia was paralyzed and made no move toward the gun at her hip. Wade fixed her with a terrible look. "Lift it!"

Slowly, she reached down and pulled the gun clear, but she couldn't level it at him.

"Ear the hammer back!" he barked.

In the process of cocking the pistol, the barrel wavered in Wade's direction. His gun slipped out with the smoothness of long practice, and he thumbed a shot as the muzzle cleared the holster. The girl was knocked backward and onto the floor—again. She reached for her left hip. It tingled with numbness. She pulled her hand away to gaze on it in half-expectant horror. When she found no blood on it, she began to pant.

Wade stepped over to her. "Get up. Get up!" She struggled to her feet clutching her side and sobbing.

"Now you know what it feels like to stare death in the face—be on the receiving end of violence. You're not hurt. I only hit the belt buckle."

The burst of the shot was still in Patricia's ears, and the room was rank with powder smoke. She stood, trembling as she faced the madman before her.

Wade said, "Get your clothes on. We're going for a ride."

The girl was finally able to exhale. "Where?"

"I don't know, but I'm taking you along for insurance. Maybe they'll think twice before they shoot you down to get me. Get dressed."

Patricia made no effort to comply. Wade whipped out his gun again and gritted, "Do I have to pistol-whip you to make you obey or do you want to go out of here in a nightgown?"

Wade saw an implacable, stubborn look fix itself to Patricia's face. Suddenly flushed, he ripped a blanket from the bed and held it before him, higher than his head. Patricia fumbled in the heaps from the drawer, found her split riding skirt, pulled it on under her nightdress and, after a quick look at the raised blanket, finished dressing.

Another door in the hallway shut quickly as they exited the room. Patricia preceded Wade down to the lobby. He slipped into the owner's office and jerked a rifle from the wall. In a drawer, he located a box of shells and stuffed them into his pockets. They walked out into the stillness of the street and across to the livery stable. At Wade's insistence, Patricia selected a horse, saddled, and mounted him. Wade picked a good one for himself and, in seconds, was saddled and up. He looked up and down the street. Keeping his pistol on Patricia, he motioned for her to ride behind the buildings then followed her out of town.

VII. Discovery

They headed for the high timber, but exhaustion was quickly dulling Wade's desire for deep cover. The trail led to a broad canyon. Its sloping walls were covered with quaking aspen, patches of stately sugar pine, and cedar. Wade looked hard down the back trail for any sign of pursuit. Pistol still drawn, he got off his horse, grabbed Patricia's reins, and led the horses into the trees.

Patricia said in a small voice, "I'd like to straighten you out on a misunderstanding. I think the Pat Laughlin you're taking me for is my uncle."

"Makes no difference to me. I'm holding onto you; I'd like to live a little longer."

"Kidnapping women is about your speed. If I ever saw a man without honor, you're him."

"Get down," Wade said, tying the horses to a tree.

"Do you know how many men you killed last night in the saloon?" Her voice wasn't small anymore. "Three! Three men you'd probably never seen before. I hear you also shot a mere boy who couldn't have been more than nineteen. You must be very proud of yourself."

Wade tied her hands and feet.

"Does it bother you to think about the two men you murdered on the trail out of Genoa?" asked Patricia. Wade fastened the rope to the same tree as the horses. If she was related to the man who was behind his troubles, he had to hold on to her.

"I see," said Patricia, squatting. Wade loosened both saddle belts, then dropped a saddle blanket on Patricia. He wrapped the other blanket around him, lay on the pine needles, and was out.

When the sun hit him, Wade turned to make sure Patricia was still there. She was sleeping in a heap, still tethered to the tree.

He studied her features. She was undeniably attractive and showed considerable spirit—a great reason not to give her any leeway.

"I don't suppose there'll be any breakfast," she said when his saddle blanket was back in place. Wade took her blanket, folded and replaced it, then returned her saddle to the horse. He untied Patricia and motioned for her to mount up.

Patricia looked around. No rescue and the country was entirely unfamiliar to her; she wouldn't know which way to run. She mounted the horse. Wade tied a line to his horse and swept into the saddle.

On top of a hogback, Wade stopped to survey the country. To the west were the sharp escarpments of the Sierras. To the east were the barren, rolling hills of the Nevada desert.

"I think I could kill someone in self-defense, but never out of malice or indifference," Patricia said as they started again. "What must that feel like?"

"You just haven't been up against the right kind of provocation," Wade said. "You and I are on different sides of the fence. Let it go at that."

"My Aunt Bella's bustle! You're the lowest vermin I've ever encountered! When a man faces you in a fair fight, you turn yellow. But, in the dark, you can shoot men down and slap women around."

He reined his horse back and turned to her. "This is wild country. Even if you were free, animals or the land itself would probably stop you before you ever found your way back to town. Still, if you try to make a break, I'll shoot you out of the saddle. Just keep close—and don't make trouble."

***

As they approached the pass, the canyon walls began to close in. Snow-covered peaks leaned toward them, and chilled air bit into lungs that worked harder in the rarefied altitude. Once over the top, they looked down into a green, mountain meadow. In the distance was a lapis blue lake. On its far shore was an Indian lodge made of white buckskin. Jagged patterns in yellow and brilliant red zigzagged along its sides. The trail down was slippery, unsettled shale. Soon it leveled, and the horses had easier going.

The figure of an American Indian squatted at the edge of the lake before the lodge. As they neared, the Indian stood and faced them. He was imposing—well over six feet—with a massive chest and broad shoulders. From under his tall-crowned hat two thick braids of graying hair fell to his dark shirt. Around the top of his pants was a magnificent belt with silver conchos studded with brilliant turquoise.

Wade raised his hand to him. The Indian grunted, looked Patricia up and down, and then said, "Where you gettum squaw? Him pretty."

"No good, no cook," said Wade. "I'll trade you for a good pack burro or a buckskin."

"White brother big fool. Give to diggers for lame horse." The Indian walked around Patricia's horse and eyed her up and down. "Squaw soft like punkwood. You win him in crap game?"

"I stole her. Now I'm gonna leave her here." Wade untied the line from Patricia's saddle. Patricia's pulse began to thump in her ears.

"Mebbe so, two dollah Mex," said the Indian.

"You don't own me!" Patricia protested.

"Mm," grunted the Indian. "Squaw not keep her tongue. You go."

Wade nudged his horse forward. "I'll go when I'm good'n ready."

The Indian drew himself up to his full height. "You leave now!"

The Indian sprang at Wade and dragged him from the saddle. They fell to the ground and rolled in a tangle of thrashing arms and legs. They rolled over small bushes and knocked over a pelt frame at the side of the lodge, emitting grunts, growls, and muffled curses as they went.

Patricia stared, her thoughts racing. The Indian didn't seem any more desirable a companion than Wade. If she was to get a break, it would have to be now, while they were distracted.

She casually tried to get her horse closer to Wade's. If she could swat the animal hard, Wade wouldn't be able to follow her, at least, not at first. But how far would she get in unfamiliar country?

Then she spied the rifle on Wade's horse. It offered her a

fighting chance. She reached with a shaky hand, but Wade's horse started, spooked as the men rolled into its legs. It quickly trotted to the other side of the lodge. Patricia shook her head, then slowly slipped from her saddle.

The big chief picked Wade off the ground. With a couple of running steps, he threw him into the lake.

Patricia closed in on Wade's horse, but it shied away, back to the other side of the lodge.

Wade came up spitting and breathless. As he waded toward shore, the Indian reached out, grasped his hand, and pulled him onto dry ground. Patricia closed on the horse. Wade pumped the Indian's hand up and down. "You old renegade, how are you?"

Patricia was reaching toward the horse's reins, but her head turned as the Indian responded.

"Fine, Wade, just fine. Looks like you've been through a meat chopper. Been playing with explosives?" asked the Indian.

"Little trouble—tangled with a horse," said Wade.

"Horse win?"

"Sure looks that way, don't it?"

"Hey," said the Indian. "What's the lady want with your mount?"

"I imagine she'd like my rifle," said Wade as his horse trotted back to the far side of the lodge. Patricia sat where she was and put her head in her hands.

"I thought maybe someday I'd grow up and be able to lick you, Chief," said Wade, shaking water out of his face.

"You gave me a tussle. I'd hate to fight you if you were really mad. Sure missed you! Remember the bear you shot to save Sam Blue? I still have the skin on the floor of my lodge. We had a fine calf crop this year. I'll start 'em down from the hills this week. Running Doe's cooking for the boys in the hay harvest." He raised a warning finger. "Don't fail to stop and see her on your way down!"

Patricia stretched her stiff legs and lay on her back, resigned. The sun's warmth relaxed her fatigued body. The two men squatted on the ground.

"How're the boys, Chief?"

The chief's face grew serious. "Black Wolf and Sam Blue are at the ranch."

"And Raven Eye?"

"He got tangled up with the wrong bunch—always was a wild one."

"He's a good Indian," Wade said consolingly. "Just a little reckless and restless, that's all. He's like me—he never liked routine. He'll straighten out."

The old chief shook his head. "Too late, Wade. The tribe put the sign on him. He will die. I sat at the council fire and voted with the rest. I have only two sons now."

Wade looked down, then threw a stone into the lake. The old Indian studied the younger man intently, and his weathered features clouded. He reached into his pocket and pulled out a peculiarly-shaped gold nugget. It was elongated and tapered like a pollywog and had a gold ring embedded in the small tip. "You know this? Your father wore it for a watch fob." Wade took the nugget and stared. "He was a good man, Wade. I'm afraid he met bad medicine."

"Where did you get it?"

"On the Little Beaver west of the forks. Saw it shining in a riffle as I made the crossing."

"Do you remember the exact spot?" The old chief gave him a look and Wade said, "Sorry. Dumb question. You were his friend. Could you show me?"

"I'm all set—been expecting you. What took you so long?"

"A little trouble in Gardnerville. We could sure use some grub," he said nodding to Patricia.

"I've got that, and extra blankets and jerky for the trail," added the chief.

"Have you got any tooth powder?" asked Wade, cupping a hand to smell his own breath.

The chief smiled and nodded. "At least I got you to take a bath!" He turned to Patricia and said, "We'll have you fixed up in a lamb's shake, ma'am."

Patricia took the occasion to wet her kerchief in the lake and mop her face and neck.

They were soon fed and riding down the trail with Patricia in front. "What," asked the chief, "makes the squaw so unhappy?"

Wade outlined the rumors on the grapevine that a certain Pat Laughlin was behind his troubles—and every other rancher's. "I nearly killed her before I found out she has the same name as her uncle. She talks holier-than-thou, but she's mixed up in this somehow."

"She may be more trouble with you."

"I had to bring her; figured I might use her if I met up with the gang that was after me. They had me all set for a hanging before I got away."

"They'll comb the brush for you now."

"Can't help it. They've been combing it anyway."

"You'd better turn her loose, Wade. She'll only be a burden to you."

"She'd never find her way back from here. I may sneak down a ways until I can put her on a trail that will lead her to town." The chief only smiled. "Maybe bringing her was a fool's errand. I was a little loco after the beating I took. I was so crazy, I'd have shot my best friend if I thought he was mixed up in this stuff."

They rode over ridges and twisted down into murky canyons to wind up a narrow trail to another ridge. As they rode under a huge sugar pine, a deafening sound exploded in their ears. The horses shied, and Patricia almost dropped her reins. A flock of wild pigeons had burst out of the tree over her head. The reaching hammer of a hundred wings in labored flight was like thunder breaking the still air. The birds circled, then disappeared with astonishing speed over a nearby ridge.

The trio camped on the west fork of the Carson and were up at the crack of dawn. Patricia saw to her own horse.

"Leave the horses," said the chief. "We'll go in on foot." He carried a gold pan and a short-handled shovel.

"She's quite the outdoor gal," muttered the chief to Wade as they trudged along.

"And deadly, I'd wager, if we get distracted," countered Wade.

They came to a ford where the Little Beaver meets the Carson River. The chief pointed to a spot on the near shore, bottomed with fine gravel and sand. "That's where I found the nugget."

Wade dug a short trench through the sandbank but found nothing. They moved upstream until they came to a sharp turn that was loaded with driftwood and other flotsam. It was Patricia who spied the white object caught in the limbs of a half-submerged willow. They dug it out and found it to be the skull of a burro. There was nothing distinctive about it, so they proceeded upstream. At the next bend the chief pointed to another white object. It proved to be the humerus bone of a burro.

A leg bone and skull from a burro might have some significance. They resumed the search until Wade saw something odd crammed in the crotch of another tree. "A boot?"

Patricia wanted to laugh. "How would a boot . . ." She fell silent at the expressions on the men's faces.

The trail was hot. Wade climbed the bank and looked upstream. About four hundred feet farther up, in another sharp bend, was a steep cutbank of red sandstone and clay.

They moved to this spot, and Wade dug again. This time they took a shovelful of sand down to the creek and slowly washed it in the gold pan. Soon a sediment of black sand was all that was left in the pan, at least, at first glance. Sprinkled in with this sand was the unmistakable glitter of fine particles of gold. Wade tried another load of sand. After a couple more pans full, an object panned out that was not gold.

It was greenish-black. Wade picked it out and examined it closely. "Do you figure like I figure?" he asked, handing the corroded brass .44-caliber cartridge case to the chief.

"I'm way ahead of you. I thought as much the day I found your dad's watch fob. Seems like a long shot for a coincidence, but remember the old trail to the Jason mine crosses just above here. If he was bushwhacked and a cutbank was caved in on top of him, there are a number of things that could have washed down in two years of rains."

"Long talk for you," said Wade soberly.

"He was packing a train of high grade," said the chief. "He must have been jumped. He made a run for it and holed up near here. No mystery—just a question of where and who."

They walked slowly up the creek with keen eyes searching and probing. Again, it was Patricia who pointed. They pulled a patch of weathered cloth out of the sand where it lay half-buried. It proved to be a tattered piece of a shirt. Farther on they found a wad of stiff, dehydrated leather that was once a leather jacket.

"That was a present from Running Doe," said Wade bitterly. "I remember the Christmas when he got it." He held it for a moment as memories softened the expression on his face.

A bleached bone was their next find—and it wasn't the bone of a burro. The chief pulled it out and said, "Here. I'll dig up under the bank."

Wade and Patricia stood back while the chief plied the shovel. The sand and dirt piled up. The chief stopped with the shovel poised. The shovel descended slowly, and they could hear the grate of metal as he scraped on something with care. He put the shovel down. After a few more sweeps with his hands, the chief slowly stood—not to his full height—his chin on his chest. He raised his head until he stared straight into the sky. He lifted his arms with palms spread in supplication to the Great Spirit.

***

Wade, eager and reluctant, moved toward the chief. With some effort he forced his eyes to the shallow pit. One quick glance, and he turned his head to stare off across the blue distance. His eyes were fixed and unseeing. His face was putty-colored.

Wade felt moisture on his battered cheek and was surprised to find tears. His chest constricted, as though he were holding his breath. He felt a convulsion of his diaphragm, and he heard a wracking, moaning sob that seemed to come from somewhere behind him. He sat abruptly, sick and nauseated. He could hardly control the retching jerk of his gut. Head between his knees, he sat hunched as mental pictures of what must have happened to his father made his pain more acute. Knowledge came to him that he had only considered dimly before. There had always been a deep tie of sameness between him and his father. Now, after these years of separation, he finally saw it. Not shining icons, just men.

He rose to his feet and wiped the tears from his face. His hands came slowly to his sides and balled into tightly clenched fists. Hot thoughts of vengeance—trooping into his mind like unbidden devils—transformed his countenance from sadness to a grimace of hate as feral and deadly as a trapped timber wolf. He kicked the shovel, sending it into the rocks where it spanged loudly. He picked up a clod of dirt and flung it to the ground, then splashed into the creek and up the other bank, smashing at impeding branches and tearing up sage clumps as he went. He stopped on a knoll and glared at the world around—as though he would take out his animus on the very elements.

"This was Wade's father," said the chief for Patricia's benefit, but still staring after Wade. Then he added, mostly to himself, "Some men have too little devotion to their pas, others too much. We don't seem to get it right until it's too late."

Now Patricia's stare was as intent as the chief's. She seemed to study Wade.

Finally, Wade gained control of himself and walked slowly down into the creek toward the chief. He picked up the shovel. He saw compassion in the chief's eyes and turned dumbly away. He walked to a spot near a tree high on the hill and began to dig.

The chief took off his dark woolen shirt and began his grisly task. As he carried the shirt-wrapped bundle up the hill, it made a dull, sickening sound. Patricia waited on the bank.

The chief placed the bundle in the hole Wade had prepared. He took off his silver and turquoise-studded belt and laid it on top of the shirt. He and Wade filled in the grave and made a little cairn of stones to mark the spot.

After the burial, the chief headed for the spot where the body had been found. He dug up against the bluff, hoping to find a pistol or rifle. Suddenly, he dropped down on his knees and peered at the side of the trench. "Wade! Look."

Wade squatted down and peered into the shallow hole. On the wall of the bluff scratched into the sandstone by a gun sight were three letters: BRI.

The chief stood. "The killer leaves a brand? He was too careless, too sure."

"Maybe," said Wade.

VIII. Blood

They parted at their campsite. The chief went back up the mountain to his sheep camp; Patricia and Wade followed a trail down toward Gardnerville. Both were so engrossed in their own thoughts that they didn't hear the other rider approaching until he was almost on them. They were crossing a small meadow, high with willows, when a sharp turn in the trail brought him into full view. Patricia brought up her horse sharply and spoke one word, "Calhoun!"

Coming from behind, Wade pulled his gun as he rounded the turn. With both hands on the pommel of his horse, Bridger looked the two over. His smile was pleasant. He was apparently in good humor. "So there you are. I wondered what had become of you. We've missed you. Were you kidnapped by this cowpoke?"

Patricia said, "This man—and I use the term loosely—has held me prisoner for nearly two days."

Wade began to tremble. He clamped his jaws together and executed every force of his will to keep control of himself. His mouth tasted sour. He said softly, "Get off of your horse, Bridger."

Bridger grinned. "Brave, aren't you, when you're hiding behind a woman's skirts? Why don't you just shoot me in the guts right now? You didn't have the nerve to draw on me in Carson, but I expect you're yellow enough to shoot me down when you have the drop."

"Step down, Calhoun," said Wade.

The heavier man swung to the ground and hung his belt and gun on the saddle horn. "Now can't we talk this over like gentlemen? After all, I'm naturally interested in Miss Laughlin's welfare. She's been left in my care, and I feel responsible for her. See, I've been very concerned since the sheriff is looking for you for killing four men—or was it six? Tsk, you're such a hellion; I've really lost count. Enough to hang you though, that I guarantee."

Wade's eyes were fixed on his opponent.

"And if the sheriff doesn't find you, Whitey Cross will. You've heard of Whitey Cross. He's only the fastest gun between Sonora and the Canadian. Salty Burrows was his best friend. Salty's dead, you know, killed while trying to leave a saloon. And High-Pockets Rafferty, he just loves you! High-Pockets used to be quite a ladies' man. Know what you did? Shot his ear and half his face away."

Wade swung down from the saddle with gun leveled. "Back up towards me, Mister. Move!" Bridger complied, and Wade reached out a hand. "No shoulder holster? No boot hideout, no derringer, or knife in the shirt? 'Fraid you're slipping. It's recommended in the latest fiction: what the well-dressed villain should wear."

44

Bridger stood docilely while Wade searched him. "We don't hold well with making war on women in this country. You know, there are forty men in these hills just itching to get you in hand. And they will, I guarantee it."

With amazing speed Bridger swung an arm backward and batted Wade's gun aside as it exploded. Spinning, he drove a fist into Wade's face. The gun flew out of Wade's hand as he fell on the trail with a jarring impact—flat on his back.

Wade was stunned. Bridger jumped at his face with boot heels churning and driving. Wade writhed and rolled to one side. He grabbed a foot and twisted until Bridger dropped. Each clawed himself up his rival, slapping down blows until they were on their feet, Bridger throwing blows to Wade's face and Wade hammering Bridger's body. Bridger brought a knee to Wade's groin, but Wade turned sideways and caught it on the thigh, swinging the sharp point of an elbow into Bridger's face. Wade met a vicious one-two to the head that set him rocking back on his heels. Blood flowing from his nose, Bridger tried to stomp on Wade's instep as Wade grabbed him with an arm lock and threw him through the air with a flying mare.

Still on his feet, Bridger lowered his head, charged, and took a wicked right to the stomach, still managing to clamp Wade in a bearlike grip. He squeezed until his own face turned dark. The pressure made Wade's temple veins stand like cords. He roweled Bridger mercilessly in the calf. Bridger threw him away with an oath and closed in again with a twisting headlock.

Wade reached up over Bridger's shoulder and hooked a hand under his chin while striking him behind the knee with the other hand. He exerted pressure under the chin until the headlock was broken. He lifted the sagging Bridger, smashing him to the ground, then dropped on him hard with both knees, aiming an elbow to the side of the neck. But Bridger bucked and sent him sprawling. Bridger landed on him with a hard-driving right fist, which Wade caught with a forearm. He seized Bridger's hair and butted him in the face. Bridger got a driving knee to the solar plexus, but grappled Wade, forcing his arms against his body.

They locked together like two fighting snakes, writhing, cursing, tugging, gasping for air—even biting each other in their fury—and smearing each other with their own blood and sweat. They rolled into the brush, knocked down willow clumps, and broke sage brush. They tussled under the horses, bumping nervous, dancing hooves.

Fatigue glazed their eyes as they stood toe-to-toe and traded punches with pitiful efforts at defense. All finesse was gone from their fighting. Bridger had fought in tough camps in six states. He knew all the tricks and had the weight and strength to stand up to the best. But now, for the first time, he felt himself giving ground. He rallied his remaining strength, but found his arms like lead, his lungs were on fire, and he was unconscious of feeling in his legs.

Wade kept boring in with forearm muscles rigid. He drove each punch home with a twist of the body and the force of his thighs. Bridger's guard dropped lower. He rolled his head to ride out the vicious blows. Blood and saliva drooled from his mouth and stained his shirt. Sheer, stubborn instinct kept him up until his legs would no longer support him. He sank to his knees as Wade's sinewy hands encircled his throat. Wade dug his thumbs into the windpipe and applied pressure until Bridger's tongue protruded and his face turned a dark purple.

Patricia had sat during the entire spectacle. Her expression wasn't so much one of fear; she looked more like a judge weighing a prisoner's guilt. Now she dropped from her horse, shouting at Wade.

"You're killing him. Let him go! Let go," she screamed, grabbing his hair, but unable to pull him off. She spied the gun and belt on Bridger's saddle. Scrambling, she snatched the heavy piece from the holster and pointed it at Wade.

"Let go, you cowardly sidewinder, or I'll blow your head off!"

Wade didn't look up. His eyes, crimson and set in a face mashed beyond the point of looking human, never ceased to glare at the purple visage before him.

Patricia raised the gun barrel and rapped him sharply over the head. Wade hardly blinked. She took the barrel in both hands and brought down the butt with all her strength. She saw the scalp split—but Wade maintained his grip. She shuddered as she raised the gun high this time. Before she could bring it down again, Wade's fingers slipped from Bridger's throat and he toppled over sideways. Bridger fell face down in the trail.

Patricia dropped the gun. She looked at the two men lying as still as death. She knew she must somehow get them separated before one of them came to. Bridger moaned. She stood over him and saw normal color coming back into his face. His eyes slowly opened, and he looked up at her with a belligerent snarl. As complete consciousness returned, he recognized her and moved a hand helplessly. With her help he managed to struggle to his knees, where he swayed, waiting for strength.

Patricia got him to his feet and led him, staggering, down the trail. She left him for a moment and went back for the horses. Bridger hooked a big arm over a saddle horn and continued down the trail, supported by the horse. Patricia finally spied a large rock. Positioning a horse beside it, she guided Bridger to step up and mount the animal.

They went about two miles when another rider came up the trail. The rider was Whitey Cross, Bridger's right-hand man. Cross nodded curtly to Patricia and turned to Bridger. His brow furrowed at the sight. "The boys haven't cut his trail below."

"Up at Willow flat," said Bridger breathlessly. "He had Patricia hostage. We left him lying up there."

"Dead?"

"Don't think so."

"You mean you left him . . . alive?"

"I was hardly in a position to do otherwise." Bridger would have spat it out with more venom, had he enough air in his lungs. "Patricia got me out."

"Looks like he tied you up and worked you over with a club. You're sure a mess, man."

"Gotta' give the devil his due. He laid a gun on me. I jumped him and he whipped me good. Never thought I'd take such a beating," he paused for breath, "in any kind of a fight."

"Well he ain't immune to lead poisoning," said Whitey. Now remembering Patricia, he added, "If he harmed Miss Laughlin at all, he's a dead pigeon."

"She's been with him since the fight in the saloon."

"If the mangy co-yote is still up there, I'll get him." Whitey's horse spurted into a plunging run up the trail.

Patricia and Bridger headed for the ranch.

IX. Distraction

Wade sat up and felt his pounding head. His hand came away with sticky, half-congealed blood. He looked around until he found his gun. It was filled with grit and weeds. He wiped it dumbly on his pants, then staggered to the horse and lurched aboard.

"What a mess!" he muttered. These doings weren't exactly respectful of his face. It might never get a chance to heal, he thought. It was getting a little monotonous.

He was more than glad to be free of Patricia. Dragging her around was no help to his cause; it was a crazy notion from the first. Still, the little cuss had spunk. He managed a smirk as he felt his pistol-whipped head. He was dizzy as he moved up the trail. As he passed a large clump of sage, he heard a voice give a sharp, harsh command behind him.

"Hold it, Forester!"

If he had had the strength, Wade would have rolled his eyes. He let his gun hand flop back negligently on the horse's hip as he turned toward the owner of the raucous voice. A man with a gun trained on him rode out of the brush into the trail behind him. He was a small-boned man with two yellow buckteeth sticking almost straight out from his upper lip. His face had the putty-like appearance of one addicted to drugs. His eyes protruded bulbously—the irises so small, they made the whites seem all the larger. Most startling was the pink around his pupils, and the whiteness of his hair and his eyebrows. His face advertised a wicked intent.

"Wait up there, bud," he said with clipped speech, assessing the damage of the fight. "I want a word with you."

"I'm listenin'."

"Just thought I'd let you know who was gunnin' you down and why."

"Save it, you albino rat. I already know. You're Whitey Cross."

"The same. Glad I don't have to draw you a diagram."

"Nope. Are you going to give me an even break or just slaughter me?"

Whitey's voice raised high. "Give you an even break! Salty didn't get no break from you. Who do you think you are?" He leaned forward. "Do you think you're good enough to match me? Whi-tey Cross, remember?"

"I remember. You have a reputation. The only man I ever saw you kill was a kid in the Mad Dog Saloon in Virginia City. You goaded him to move and then murdered him."

"He was nothin'. I've matched some real fast guns in my time."

"And you've bushwhacked men that were your betters too."

As they talked, Wade touched his horse with his left spur, on the side away from Whitey. The horse grew restless and moved its front feet from side to side. There was a rifle in the boot on the left side of the saddle. Wade shifted his right hand from the hip to the horse's neck and patted him as though to still him. While his hand was in that position, he worked the rifle lever with his left hand. He swore loudly at the horse to mask the click as the breech snapped home.

Whitey contemptuously sheathed his gun, hoping Wade would make a foolish move from his awkward position. "You talk tough for a dead man."

"You'd better take me to Bridger," said Wade. "I've got a few things to tell him that he might like to know."

"For instance?"

"Like the whereabouts of David Laughlin—Patricia's father—and her Uncle Pat."

"You know where they are?" asked Whitey through narrow eyes.

"I know they haven't been seen around these parts for nearly a month."

"The old man's dead. I cooled him myself."

"Where? How'd—"

"A while back—under Bridger's orders—so there's nothing to tell Mr. Cal-houn. He already knows," Whitey said for emphasis.

"I can't stand up to you in a fair shoot-out so, if you kill me, it will have to be in cold blood."

Wade lifted his right hand from the horse's neck and used both hands to unbuckle his gun belt. He let it drop, but it was held to his leg by the thong that tied at the bottom. He didn't have to feign exhaustion while reaching with his right hand, as though to untie the thong. As he did so he nudged the horse lightly with his spur, and it swung around until the rifle pointed directly at Whitey. Wade continued his downward motion as he triggered the rifle with his left hand, a blast of fire spurting from the tip of the leather gun case. Wade hit the ground and swung the horse between him and Whitey, pulling the .30 from the boot.

As the .30 exploded, Whitey whipped his gun out and snapped a shot at Wade. It went wild. Whitey's horse reared and screamed as the .30 slug hit it in the chest. Whitey slid from the saddle and tried another shot. His horse pitched over on its side, leaving Whitey exposed. He tried to flatten out behind his horse, but a slug took him in the stomach. He rolled on the ground.

Wade's gun and belt still dragged on the ground. He buckled it to his lean waist and hobbled to where Whitey Cross lay. After looking at him for a moment, Wade turned back to his horse and mounted once again. Those shots would likely bring other riders, so it was time he was hightailing it out of there.

As he rode, his mood became morose. Another dead man. He was tired of killing and running and looking for cover like a rabbit. He came to a cross trail and turned north. After an hour's ride, he looked on the rich meadowland of the chief's homestead.

In a corner of the field opposite the ranch house, he saw several figures working around the skeletal form of a hay stacker tripod. A wagon load of hay pulled up, and the hay hook dropped down from the stacker boom, as the power team was backed up by its Mexican driver. The team moved out, and the load soared up and over the rising stack. A quick jerk of the rope, and the load fluttered down to be judiciously evened out by two men atop the stack.

To Wade, this was a familiar scene. As a boy he had driven the power team or shuttled back and forth from the fields with a hayrack. At fourteen he would spend from dawn to dark in the hayfields. In the winter, he climbed the stacks and pitched hay down to the hungry cattle.

As he rode into the stack yard, he was hailed from the top of the stack. "We don't need any help from drifters. Move on; there's no grub line here."

Wade frowned up at the owner of the voice and said, with

some asperity, "And who asked you for a job or a hand-out? Your manners are worse than your haying; never saw such a wobbly stack. What are you doing mixing hay with fire water anyway?"

The owner of the voice grabbed a guy cable with gloved hands and came sliding down from the stack, kicking toward Wade's head as he flew by. Wade dismounted, and the two men faced each other, their faces wreathed in grins.

"How ya been, Black Wolf—you old chuckwalla?" Wade said as they gripped hands.

"Fat, Wade, fat and rolling in clover. Looks like you been in some dirty saloon, letting toddlers kick the snot out of you."

"I'm bushed, beat, and have a bear of an appetite."

"That mashed up mug nearly made you unrecognizable. The other guy must need a doctor—or a mortician."

"*They're* wearing my brand."

"Shorty Bolton was by. Rumor has it you had a little party in Gardnerville. Must be stifling for you in this country—trying to find recreation, I mean."

"I wasn't bored."

"I'd have given a mink pelt to've been there; you were always lucky at digging up excitement!"

A look of consternation and fear spread over Wade's face. He ran his hand down his temple and whirled around, looking at nothing in particular.

"What's the matter? You look like you lost something important."

"Such a *stupid*, blind—"

"What?"

"Have you got two good horses you'd be willing to let die?"

"I don't get it."

"The chief's in mortal danger. I didn't realize it until the girl got away. I was groggy from a beating, then Whitey Cross jumped me. I was spent, couldn't think after that."

Black Wolf swung up behind Wade with one quick leap and said, "Head for the barn. I've got fresh horses."

The sorrel stretched out with his double load. Sweeping up to the corral, they flung themselves from the saddle. Black Wolf was over the fence and, in seconds, had two mounts ready.

X. Slaughter

Wade and Black Wolf pulled up their mounts at the top of a ridge. Wade said, "We've got to give the horses a breather. They look like they just came out of a river."

"Your head needs sewing."

Wade touched the now caking, but still oozing, blood and winced. "My head needs a lot more than that!"

"What's happened with the chief?"

"We found my dad's body. The girl was with us. We also found the letters *BRI* scratched on the cutbank. If the girl saw it, she might have made it known to Bridger, intentionally or otherwise."

"So he'll figure to get you and the other witness."

"If I'm wrong, it's been a tough, fast ride. If I'm right . . . Let's go!"

The horses labored again, their nostrils flared and red. On the steepest pitches the two riders would dismount and trot beside the horses. Near the pass they resorted to the whip and spur as the horses staggered and reeled on spent legs. Black Wolf's horse went down and lay inert until a compassionate bullet ended its life.

Wade stepped down and stripped the gear from his mount, which stood with head down and weary legs quivering. "If we could cool him down, he might make it."

"Whose horse is it? Shoot him and stop wasting time!" The Indian was already jogging up the trail. From the top of the ridge they sprinted down the other side toward the lake and the lodge on the opposite side. The quiet was ominous. As they reached the lodge, Black Wolf called once in his native tongue, but there was no answer.

"He's probably out with the sheep," said Wade; but his eyes showed desperation.

"He was to have kept them in close because we were moving them down tomorrow." Black Wolf's countenance was dark. "You look over that lower ridge. I'll scout above."

In a matter of minutes, Wade let out a shrill yell, and Black Wolf darted out of the brush above to join him. They stood looking at a patch of flat meadowland. The area was dotted with the bodies of sheep that had been slain by rifle fire. They raced through this field of carnage toward the lip of the canyon beyond, slowing only for moment as they passed the body of a black-and-white shepherd dog.

They reached the lip of the canyon and peered into its depths. Below them were the stacked bodies of sheep that had been driven over the cliff. They proceeded along the cliff rim, eyes probing into the brush and rocks at the bottom. They came to the body of another dog that had been gut shot with a high-powered rifle.

"Old Calico," said Black Wolf. "Best damn sheepdog to ever

herd a flock." Looking from the dog to the ridge, he said, "He was dragging his guts a hundred feet to get to something—and it wasn't the sheep!"

The ridge rose to a huge slab of granite that broke off and dropped perpendicular to the canyon floor three hundred feet below. Wade peered over the edge of the bluff and motioned for Black Wolf to come. They body of the chief lay in a bed of broken boulders and jagged rocks. They ran around the granite slab to the shale slide beyond, slipping and sliding their way to the bottom where they stopped beside the chief. Wade squatted and touched a coppery fist that still held a wisp of curly brown hair in its grasp. He felt a wide, guilt-laden canyon open violently inside him.

Black Wolf looked down, a softness bathing his features. There were no tears, but his eyes reddened and darkened and his skin became flushed. A grim expression gradually distorted his features. He slowly drew a knife from its scabbard and whetted its ten-inch blade on a nearby slab of shale.

They carried the chief's broken body up to the lodge and gently laid it on the bear skin. Black Wolf rounded up three horses. They put the chief's saddle on one and placed his blanket-wrapped form across the saddle. He and Wade rode bareback to the place they had ridden their horses to death. In saddles once more, they headed for the home ranch. Running Doe would clothe the chief in the finest beaded buckskin. He would wear the long war bonnet of a great chief on his journey to the Great Spirit.

The ranch house was a solid-looking affair with log walls and a huge, fieldstone fireplace at the north end. A commodious front porch with a shake roof afforded protection from the rain and sun. Running Doe had seen the trio coming across the hayfields and met them at the door. Her colorful dressing gown was broken up by her long, gray-streaked braids. They carried the chief in and laid him on his bed.

Wade said nothing. He couldn't look at Running Doe. Black Wolf handed him a blanket, and he stumbled to a cot on the enclosed back porch. He had lost both of his fathers in one day, but exhaustion forced his mind to silence.

In the morning, Running Doe touched his arm. Wade turned slowly. As he filled his mouth with the fried dodgers and goat's milk she had brought him, his eyes filled with tears.

"I'm the worst kind of a fool, Running Doe. I got the chief into this—it's my fault! I feel so . . ."

"When the wolf is loose, many sheep are slaughtered," said Running Doe. "I do not blame you for the evil of others, my son, and neither should you."

"If I'd only used my head! They moved so fast, I—"

"Your father is gone, and so is my husband. Soon the enemy will be in our backyard for my sons. They must be stopped! Black Wolf is going to war."

Wade found Black Wolf at the corral with a fresh horse saddled. A Winchester hung in a scabbard under bother stirrup leathers.

"Where do you think you're going?" asked Wade.

Black Wolf swung into the saddle with no reply.

"My father is dead too, Black Wolf. I don't want your death on my conscience."

"Many will go with me."

"Sure, you can kill a half a dozen before they get you. But with you gone, this ranch goes too. A chief doesn't forsake his tribe for personal revenge. They're scattered all along this range—you wanna see them all grubbing for roots, living on chipmunks?"

The young chief sat on his horse, gripping the pommel with both hands. He lifted the reins, then slowly let them fall. His chin dropped on his chest for several seconds. Then he straightened; dignity and a new resolution were in his bearing. "You speak well, brother. I didn't consider that now I am chief."

"Your father was a great chief. You can be a great chief."

"All right, Wade. We're in this together. What is our plan?"

"Send Sam Blue to the tribe. Bill Caldwell is still ranching beyond the east rim. Send a man you can trust over to him. Alert Shorty and the old crowd—any that are still around— and we'll make some kind of a showing. There should still be people down there that are tired of being pushed around. I'll ride up to the Jason mine and keep out of sight. We'll meet at Bear Paw Springs tomorrow night."

"Then?"

"They've got a shaky title to the K-bar. Their strong point is possession. If we can take the ranch, they'll have to get us out by force or prove in court that they have a better claim than I have."

XI. Homecoming

After Bridger's fight with Wade, he took Patricia to the ranch house. "Dave—I mean your father—should be home in a day or two," he had told her as she helped him to the couch. It took all her strength just to ascend the stairs. As bone-tired as she was, she could hardly sleep; thoughts of the last few days kept her mind racing. And she couldn't wait to see her father. Exhaustion finally overtook her.

She awoke in a good mood, if not entirely rested. The morning was nearly spent, and she was hungry. Bridger was waiting for her in the kitchen. His face was a patchwork of puffy purple and burgundy, and when he spoke, he was careful about moving his jaw. "Good morning. I hope you got some rest."

"Yes, thank you." Patricia sucked air between her teeth as she looked closely at Bridger's face. "I hope you're not too sore."

"I'll be just fine."

"Is my Uncle Pat around?"

"Oh, he stays in Gardnerville most of the time."

"I would have liked to have known that when I was there at the hotel, Mr. Calhoun."

"My apologies, it's just that he was in Virginia City with your father . . . I wasn't sure whether he was back. He still may be up there with your father." He handed her a plate of eggs and toast. "Hey, how about a ride after breakfast?"

"I'm a little saddle sore," she admitted. "But maybe a ride will loosen me up."

As they jogged along the trail, it was pleasant to see many different migrant birds in flight. Wild ducks pumped by on strong wings. Occasionally they heard the ghostly call of high-flying geese. The mountains beyond were gashed with ravines filled with the blood of red leaves.

Bridger finished a lurid tale of a mining camp incident as they topped a knoll. They dismounted to stretch their legs. Patricia had been quiet and preoccupied for the last several minutes. Bridger turned to her and said, "What's knocking around in that pretty head—or can you tell me?"

Patricia wasn't quite sure what was bothering her. She was elated at the prospect of seeing her father again, but there was a hollow in her that she couldn't traverse. Finally, she said, "I think it's just all the excitement and stress. I'll be myself again soon."

Bridger said softly, "Pat, you probably . . . well, I . . . I'm in love with you. I want to marry you." Without pausing, he said, "I can't offer you much right now, but when your father's plans are realized, I stand to do very well."

Patricia gave him a quizzical look. "I knew you'd taken a liking to me," she said. "I'd be blind not to see it. We've known each other a very short time—though I've certainly come to admire your qualities. I don't think I'm in love with you. But, who am I to say that won't happen. Shouldn't we give it a little time?"

"Of course," he agreed. "I don't want to rush you into anything. I just couldn't help telling you my feelings. When the time comes, I can easily get an annulment . . ." Patricia was watching the ducks. "But there's something else on your mind."

"I'm sorry," she said. "I feel strangely depressed. I don't know why."

"I do."

"Oh?"

Bridger was diplomatic. "You have a natural tenderness. Thoughts of death and killing are revolting to you—and yet, you're worried about Wade Forester."

"Why do you say that?"

"I'm no fool." Now he was blunt. "The man intrigues you. Some of the most vicious criminals have sharp minds and fascinating personalities. Wade makes his personality felt wherever he is. I've seen his effect on others. It can be hard to reconcile it with his murderous disposition. Your question—that you won't even admit to yourself—is whether or not he's still alive."

Patricia thought that over for several seconds. "After what he did to me, I feel contempt for him. At the same time, I hope Whitey didn't finish him off. I don't want vengeance. I just don't want anyone else to die, not even him. Is that strange?"

"Whitey Cross is dead."

Patricia exhaled loudly.

"Hm," was the only sound from Bridger.

"I don't understand how anyone can take another life—let alone several," Patricia finally said. "It was all I could do to rap Forester over the head when he was strangling you."

"I won't forget that, I assure you," Bridger said. "Shall we go back?"

"Yes," she said, rubbing her lower thighs.

Patricia bounded into the ranch house. But her father wasn't there. So she went out again on foot. A shortness of breath kept ambushing her, but she needed to keep moving. When she finally headed back to the house, it was late. There was a light in the window of the big front room. A ranch hand materialized out of the darkness.

"We were about to go looking for you, Miss Laughlin," he said. As he turned his horse back to the barn, Patricia felt a hammering in her chest. She alighted on the steps with a certainty that her father had arrived.

It would be good to finally see him after nearly two years. She entered the spacious living room with the huge fireplace, and a peculiar thought struck her. This was Wade's home. These were the surroundings in his mind when he thought of home. Why should that occur to her just now?

Bridger came in from a side door and said in a whisper, "He's here. He came across country—still not feeling back to normal. He wanted to stretch out and rest and fell sound asleep. Come."

Patricia followed him down a short hall. Bridger stood to one side of a door to let her peek in. A lamp with the wick turned low was on a table beside a couch. In the feeble light she could distinguish the familiar features of her father, lying on his back with a blanket over him.

Bridger called softly, "Mr. Lau—"

Patricia seized his arm, whispering, "Don't wake him. We'll visit when he gets up."

XII. Clash

The next day at sunset, ranchers and Indians began to trickle into the clearing below Bear Paw Springs. By nine o'clock there were thirty horses in a temporary rope corral. The men were dressed more or less alike in faded jeans, denim jackets, or cowhide coats. The Indians wore beaded or concho-studded buckskin or denim with silver-tipped belts.

After some heated and flowery language was exchanged about the state of things, the men were in the saddle, following Wade down toward the K-bar. A partial moon shone as they rode into a long canyon that gradually widened into the valley.

Far out on the valley floor could be seen a few dark, shadowy blobs that were the K-bar buildings. There was the click of steel against steel as each man checked his weapons. Topping a rise, Black Wolf kneed his horse over to Wade's side and pointed to the southeast. A body of twenty-odd horsemen approached from the valley before them. Wade pulled up sharply.

"Laughlin's horsemen," he said. Looking behind them, they watched another group swarm over a ridge to cut off their retreat over the back trail. It was a neatly executed trap.

Wade had been so intent on executing his surprise attack that he forgot to put out flankers or send scouts ahead. He knew better and now cursed himself a fool who could be leading his friends to their deaths.

The horsemen approaching from the valley were in no hurry. They walked their horses up the shallow canyon floor.

"That's it," said Wade. "Thanks for everything, boys. It's me they want. They can't hold all of us. I'll ride down and give myself up. I don't think they'll bother with the rest of you."

Cursing an oath, Bill Caldwell said, "Do you think they planned this just to capture you? Don't be a fool. This is what they've been praying for—a chance to smash every man that ever crossed them or fought their mighty scheme. I say we fight!"

Black Wolf said, "He's right, Wade. This is for keeps, whether we want it that way or not. If we try to surrender or scatter, they'll slaughter us."

Wade stood high in his stirrups and looked back over the little army. "Does everyone feel that way?" There was a chorus of vehement assents—and curses.

Wade said, "Okay. Bill, you ride on my right. Black Wolf, you stay on my left. Sam Blue, pile off and give us a hand."

Black Wolf's brother Sam was only nineteen, but there was a reckless excitement in his eyes.

"Bill, tie your rope to the saddle horn," directed Wade. "Sam, pass that rope under the belly of Bill's horse and hand it to me. Good. Black Wolf, do the same thing with your rope. Sam, under his horse and up to me." Wade tied both ropes to his saddle horn.

"Keep the rope coiled in your hands, you two. Don't let it snag on anything. When I give the word, ride out and away from me. We'll start slow, then hit them at a run. Keep spread out and hold your fire until I start shooting. When I do, open fire on the middle of their ranks and close in. Don't stop to fight. These ropes should down a few horses and, hopefully, allow us through. If you make it, ride like heck out of here and scatter, got it?"

As the group of riders above them closed in at a smart canter, Wade and the others walked their horses calmly toward the group coming toward them from the canyon. No one spoke. The air was crisp and, in the moonlight, the breath of the horses spouted vapor like so many dragons. There was the rattle of bits, a tinkle of spur rowels, the creak of leather, and the steady clomp, clomp of the advancing horses, less than a thousand yards off.

At once the enemy in front spurred their horses into a running charge—this was unexpected. "Better still," shouted Wade to Bill and Black Wolf. "Rein over, rein over!" The two outside horses swerved out toward the sides, opening up like a fan. Wade drew his gun. Just before the clash, Wade's crowd fell in behind him. Bill and Black Wolf had paid out all the rope, now fiddle-string tight, among the three horses.

Wade fired into the oncoming horde. The rest let loose with pistol and rifle. The oncoming horses struck the taut rope. Some went down. Others lost their footing and swerved to one side. Bill's horse stumbled—thrown off balance by the impact. Wade's sorrel was pulled sideways, tried to rear, and fell over to the right. Wade's bunch was clubbing and shooting a path through this wash of horses and men. Wade kicked loose from the stirrups, pulled a Winchester from the boot, and used it as a club, fighting his way on foot. A downed horse reared up in front of him, and he swung to its back as it regained its feet.

There was a melee of tangled men and horses. Indians yipped and shouted as they fought. Gradually, horse after horse broke through and galloped away from the fight. Wade sighted Black

Wolf and converged on his course. They swept over a ridge together and charged into a canyon. They quartered across the other slope and headed for higher country. After two miles of this, they stopped to give their horses a breather.

Wade said, "How'd we make out?"

"Hard to say. I saw Bill's horse go down. I think they got him. Sam Blue wasn't there to pick me up. Looks like you and I both changed mounts."

"We hurt them as much or more than they hurt us. I counted twenty-five riders digging out of there, including us. We only lost four or five. That's better than I'd hoped for."

"That rope trick did it, Wade, fowled them up so bad they couldn't get started. Besides, they mistimed their charge! They thought the bunch above was close enough to close in before we got through. Sure hope Sam made it. Gray Owl tried to settle a private feud—always was a little trigger-happy. He got his chance. Just too darned headstrong to be careful."

"They almost had us boxed in. Sure glad I wasn't the only one guilty of overconfidence—but we've got a Judas among us. That ambush was too well planned and timed."

"It's not hard to figure out the leak."

"Yeah? Who was it?"

Black Wolf gave Wade a blank look. Finally he said, "Forget it. That score is mine to settle."

Wade studied Black Wolf, but only said, "We'd better split up. I'll meet you tomorrow morning below Blue Slide on the trail to Mud Lake."

"Should I get the boys together again for another try?"

"No use now. They'll have guards on the ridges and enough men in the ranch house to fight off an army. I'll tell you my idea in the morning."

XIII. Empty

Patricia had arisen and dressed hurriedly. When she got downstairs, she found that all the men, including her father, were gone.

"Where is everyone?"

"They all left," said the cook. "Big trouble." She couldn't make sense of it, but the cook had no more information. She fiddled around the house for a couple of anxious hours until she decided to head out on horseback to see if she could find anyone. An old ranch hand met her in the barn. "I don't think the lady should go out today," he said.

"But I haven't seen my father in years," she explained. "I need to find out what's going on."

The old man couldn't stop her. "At least, stay away from the hills," he said. "Go east—or north to Gardnerville—where there are other people; there's only trouble in the hills."

Promising not to go into the hills, Patricia headed out. Even if she knew her father was in the hills, her chances of finding him were pretty slim.

She headed to Gardnerville to find her Uncle Pat. She inquired at the hotel, at a house that took in boarders, and with the sheriff. No one had seen Pat Laughlin for a more than a month. Patricia was anxious to get back to the ranch, in case her father and the others had returned. But only the cook was there to greet her.

About nine o'clock that night, she finally saw a group of horsemen approaching. Bridger was in the lead. They pulled up in front of the corral and dismounted. There were four blanket-wrapped bundles across saddles. A couple of men wore head bandages, and another nursed a wounded arm.

Patricia's anxiety bloomed into panic. She ran to Bridger practically screaming, "Where is my father? Where is he?"

"Don't be alarmed," said Bridger, placating. "He didn't come in with us, that's all."

"Are you sure he isn't wrap—"

"I tell you he's all right."

"What happened? How were these men killed?"

"We expected a little trouble, went out to meet it, and got ambushed. We fought our way out, and the ambushers ran for it. Some of the boys are after them. Your father insisted that he go along. You can be proud of your father, Patricia. He has more than his share of cold nerve. He should be back any time."

"But . . . who was behind it?"

"Your friend Forester. Still pity him?"

"I can only loathe him. Why doesn't he leave the country? Why does he stay here, killing?"

"He's stubborn and smart. But I swear I'll have my hands on him soon enough."

The night dragged on with no sign of Patricia's father. Patricia and Bridger waited in the living room. At midnight they heard the faint sounds of a galloping horse. Then the tempo died down to a walk. Bridger went to the door and yelled out to the bunk house for a lantern.

Patricia saw the dim outline of a horse approaching the corral. When it reached the closed gate, it stopped. They both ran toward it as one of the men brought a lantern at a run. There was a man's body tied across the saddle. Bridger grabbed the horse by the bit and turned it around. The lantern lent an eerie light that revealed the features of David Laughlin.

XIV. Decision

Patricia's knees grew weak. She resisted the pull of the spinning ground. Bridger was quick with an arm around her. "Do you need to sit?"

"No!" she spat hoarsely.

Bridger yelled for a blanket as they gently slid the body from the saddle. As the men covered the body and carried it indoors, Bridger grabbed the light and examined the horse and blood-stained saddle.

"That's the sorrel Forester took from the livery when he kidnapped me!" said Patricia. Bridger noted the horse's blazed face and white lower legs.

"It's the same one he was riding when we fought at Willow Flat, I guarantee it."

"He's shot in the back," said one of the men from the front door.

Back in the house, Patricia collapsed on the sofa. She couldn't feel her hands or feet. At Bridger's bidding, the cook brought some tea, but she didn't want it. She wanted answers.

"Tell me what happened!"

"There's not much to tell. Wade collected a gang of riffraff and headed for this ranch. We got word in time to meet them. There was a fight, and we scattered them. Last I saw of your father, he was trying to cut off a rider that was circling back toward the hills. Looks like they ambushed him and murdered him to try to intimidate us."

"That man is kill crazy. Why haven't you stopped him?"

"You've seen what a chore that is," said Bridger. "I'm sorry. That high country is broken, wild, and covered with brush and timber. There's a half dozen small ranches back up there. Most of the ranchers are Indian friends of Wade's. I've had my men looking for him, but I won't let them go out in twos or threes. It's too dangerous. I had him once. He won't leave this country alive. That I guaran—" Bridger looked down.

"Do you think Forester did this himself?"

"What difference does it make? He did it, or one of his crowd. Your father is just as—"

Patricia stood abruptly. "I've got to rest."

"All right. I'll have Doc McFall make arrangements for your father. I'll see you in the morning."

Patricia lay staring into the darkness of her room. She couldn't sleep and she couldn't relax. Her loss weighed on her like redwood, but its pressure was crystallizing a grim determination within her. A warped, but simple, plan emerged in her haunted mind. If Calhoun was incapable of stopping these killings, she would end them herself. She'd find Forester and bring him in. If he died in flight, so be it. She wasn't naive about her chances, but she knew that being a woman could give her an element of surprise. She also knew that guns can be great equalizers. She had lived on a ranch; she knew guns and horses and had gained some knowledge of the high country from her ride with Wade.

Three hours before dawn, Patricia slipped out of her room and made her way to the barn. She led her saddled horse to the back of the house and picked up some blankets and grub. She returned to the corral and put a lead halter on the sorrel with the blazed face and white legs.

Her first stop was the Gardnerville hotel, where she retrieved her revolver. She had her other things sent to the ranch and was soon on the trail to the high country, a ready rifle under her knee. As she rode the trail to Willow Flat, her resolve solidified, but her motive became more transparent; what she was calling justice was spurred by hatred.

She knew that above Willow Flat was the cross-canyon trail down to the chief's ranch. She reached the turn where she and Wade had left it and turned north. As dawn came she found a spot that suited her purpose. There was a small opening covered with high grass and a few clumps of sage. It was just off of the trail. She hobbled the sorrel and left him to graze in this patch.

Her next step was to find a vantage point. She found a game trail that angled upward above the main trail. From an opening on this trail she could see the sorrel below. Her hope was that, if Wade came by, he would see the horse and investigate.

Dismounting, she led her own horse into a clump of brush and tied him. She spread a blanket and sat down to wait. She spent her vigil munching on bread and jerky—and giving herself over to sadness and memories of her father.

Patricia was awakened by a sound. She saw sudden movement on the trail to her right. Someone was racing up on foot. The trim, dark-haired figure darted into the little flat and bent on the far side of the sorrel. He was probably freeing the horse of its hobbles. She cursed her nap. Now there was no time to confront Forester; he'd be gone in a second. She levered a shell into the Winchester and felt the pound of her pulse in her chest and arms. At least she could keep him from getting far. But there was a thread of doubt welling up within her. Faced with an immediate target, she was suddenly unsure what to do.

With a quick flip of a long leg, her victim was mounted. The rifle came to Patricia's shoulder. The sorrel broke into a run—headed directly toward her. The horse's head and flowing mane obscured the crouching rider. How could she wing him if she couldn't get a clean sight? Patricia's options were getting worse. She saw he would gain the main trail and disappear up the mountain. She lined the sights on a small opening that was free from brush.

The horse's head came into sight as it smashed at the trail in a lunging run. Patricia cuddled the rifle to her cheek and fixed the sights on the figure over the horse's withers. The wicked snarl of the gun coughed, then echoed against the canyon wall beyond. Horse and rider disappeared behind a clump of brush. When the horse emerged on the far side, it was riderless. It galloped up the trail.

The stillness after the shot was ominous. Still gripping the now-heavy rifle, Patricia felt nauseated. Her hands became unsteady. There was no sound from below. Was there a dead man down there? Or he was writhing in agony, pouring life's blood into the dust?

Terror gripped her. Maybe he wasn't even hit. Maybe he had dived for safety from the horse's back and was stalking her now. A wild desire to escape ballooned within her.

She scooped up the blanket and ran to her horse. Tightening the cinch and ramming the rifle into the boot, she swung up and whirled her mount. She heard a shot, and a slab of bark jumped off of a tree in front of her. The vengeful ball went whining into space. A branch snapped near her head as the air filled with the buzz of angry lead hornets battering the leaves and twigs.

XV. Confronted

Wade and Black Wolf met below the blue slide on the trail to the lake. They topped a ridge a mile beyond their meeting place and pulled up to give their horses a breather. Horse tails lashed at omnipresent flies.

As they looked across the canyon, Black Wolf jutted a finger at a rider coming down the ridge beyond on a black horse. For a moment he was obscured by brush, but he came into full view as he rode onto the lake trail. The range was vast, but Black Wolf jerked the rifle from its boot and cut down on the target. The horse pitched forward, and its rider tumbled into the dust before it. Before the Indian could take another bead, the rider sprang to his feet and disappeared behind the brush by a turn in the trail.

"Why in blazes did you do that?" demanded Wade. "That looked like Raven Eye."

"It was. I'd recognize that black stallion anywhere."

"I don't get it."

"You wanted the lying Judas who gave your raid away? Well, there he goes!"

"I'll get him. Hang back and cover me in case he surprises me."

Wade jumped his horse into a run, and Black Wolf trailed him at about a hundred yards. They passed the dead horse, then ducked as a shot rang from above. It seemed to come from around the bend. They rode forward. Wade saw a body in the trail. He caught a glimpse of a rider on the hill above. He emptied his Colt as rapidly as he could pull the trigger, but the rider disappeared.

Black Wolf was closing up, so Wade passed the prostrate form and lunged up the trail to try to cut off the rider he had fired on. As his head got higher, he saw the horse come off a side trail and dash up the lake trail ahead of him. He raised his gun, then remembered it was empty. He roweled his bay mare to quickly close the gap.

When he was close enough, he reached out and grabbed the rider. The horse beneath the prey swerved; Wade retained his grip and was pulled to the ground, dragging the rider with him.

They fell in a tangle of brush. Wade pinned the rider to the ground with a knee and twisted an arm up between the shoulder blades. Black Wolf spun off of the trail and dismounted beside him.

They were both surprised to hear a muffled feminine voice saying, "Let me go! Get off of me!"

Wade sat her up as Patricia spat dirt from her mouth. "You! You killed him!"

"Me? You know I'd never hurt anyone!" Wade broke a half smile, but he held her wrists tightly.

Black Wolf said, "If I'd known we'd be wrestling an adder, I'd have kept my distance." Waving his gun, he said, "Let her go. I won't let this bushwhacker hurt you."

Wade let her go—then dodged as Patricia's hands flew at his face. "You filthy murderer!" she shrieked as Wade grabbed her forearms. "I thought I shot you."

"Talk nice, Wade," said Black Wolf. "She's liable to get mad."

"Funny," said Wade. "Said she shot me, and she's the one that's angry."

"You killed my father, you mongrel!"

"Your father? I never even laid eyes on him!"

"You lie. How can you sit there and deny it?" Patricia's head tilted. "You've forgotten that I've seen you in action."

"Wait a minute," said Black Wolf, trying to calm the torturous emotions. "When was your father supposed to have been killed?"

"Last night, after your riders ambushed the men from the K-bar. He was shot in the back and came in on the same sorrel *Mister* Forester stole from the stable when he kidnapped me."

Patricia jerked free and scrambled backward while her words took a seat in Wade's brain. He was quickly on his feet. As Patricia indignantly dusted herself off, Wade grabbed her arm. "And you pegged me? You, the young lady who lectures on how incredible it is that any person could take another human life? Well, you've done just that." He whirled and towed her back down the trail.

Now Patricia's mind had to accommodate new information. As they arrived at the body lying in the trail, Wade said, "How does it feel?"

The remnants of rage that had bloomed in Patricia's face faded to ashen white. "I . . . Who? Who have I killed?"

"My brother," said Black Wolf somberly. "So, now that we've decided it's open season on relative-killers, it looks like you're the next target."

"I didn't know," Patricia said in a breathy voice.

"You didn't know for sure that Wade killed your father," said Black Wolf. "Yet you're ready to bushwhack him and shoot him in the back. Nice to be so right—to be judge and executioner all at once."

"But Wade killed all those men—he would have killed Mr. Calhoun if I hadn't stopped him."

"While we're talking of guilt," said Wade, "did you know the chief is dead?"

"Not the one we met at the lake . . ."

"My father," said Black Wolf. "Now Wade tells me that you told Bridger about finding his father's remains; that's why my father's dead. It seems your tongue has indirectly caused another death, even before this one."

"I don't understand," said Patricia. "I didn't tell Mr. Calhoun about what we found. I mean, I may have gotten around to it later—but it never came up, I swear!"

"Then how did he find out?" asked Wade.

"I don't know. I . . ." Patricia was mumbling now.

The figure on the ground stirred and struggled. Wade crouched over him as the Indian rolled his head back and looked up at Black Wolf. "Good shot, my brother." Blood from Raven Eye's soaked tunic had run up his neck and stained his face. "I go soon," he winced as he spoke.

"Isn't there something we can do?" pleaded Patricia with new urgency. "He looked so much like Wade—tall, dark hair, riding Wade's sorrel . . ."

Raven Eye grunted out a question. "What makes the squaw so distressed?"

"She shot you," said Black Wolf.

"Squaw?! Why?" Raven Eye coughed and trembled.

"She thought you were Wade—thinks Wade killed her old man."

"I'm not a killer," she said, unable to convince even herself. "I just . . . I wanted this all to end."

After some strained breaths, Raven Eye spoke again. "Whitey Cross killed the old man about a month ago."

"But I saw him over a bloody saddle last night," said Patricia.

"I am a dead Indian. I do not lie," said Raven Eye.

"Whitey Cross said as much to me," said Wade almost to himself. "I still don't get how Bridger knew about me finding my father in the creek bed!"

Raven Eye seemed to summon his remaining strength. With an effort he said, "I saw you leaving the Little Beaver. I backtracked you and found the grave. I . . . I told Bridger. I didn't know you'd also found evidence against him there." He breathed deeply. "I've killed my father. Now I die at the hands of a squaw. It will be straight now."

Raven Eye went silent. Wade covered him with a blanket. Patricia couldn't move. The last twenty minutes had spent her, first with rage, then revulsion, and now remorseful agony. She had taken a life—with no cause whatever. The loss of her father paled in comparison.

Wade and Black Wolf hefted Raven Eye's body over the sorrel. They mounted silently and rode up to Patricia. "You'd better get off of this mountain," said Wade in a low voice. "As your father's heir, you might take up where he left off. I don't know what your plans are, but if you pursue his course, it means war from here on. You've made an attempt on my life, which I won't forget. If I die at the hands of paid killers, remember they're yours. Keep that on your conscience, if you truly have one."

He lifted his reins then dropped them. "Another thing: if we meet again, you'll want to be very alert. I have too much at stake to let your petticoats get in my way. Next time there may be less brush—and you may be in good six-gun range."

Black Wolf led the sorrel down the trail toward the ranch. Wade rode upward, toward cover in the crags of the mountains.

Patricia eased herself against a tree and let her legs fold. She yearned for clarity—for the security of four walls, not a lone tree at her back. She resolved to never seek vengeance again, but it didn't remove the weight that pressed on her chest. Patricia cried.

XVI. Information

In Gardnerville, Patricia left her horse at the livery barn and went to the hotel. She locked herself in the bathroom. She needed to be alone. She immersed herself in the copper tub and tried to soak some of the bruises out of her aching flesh. She felt lucky to have no broken bones after having been dragged from the saddle.

As her body relaxed, her mind seemed more capable of coherent thought. She would see her father properly buried and then go back to San Francisco. In her mind it extended safety to her.

When Patricia finally dressed, she made her way to the north edge of town to confer with Doc McFall. She found the doctor at home. When he opened the door, she said, "Doctor, I believe you have my father here?"

"Won't you come in?" He ushered her into a high-ceilinged room and motioned for her to sit on a horsehair sofa. The doctor seated himself in a straight chair.

"Is, uh, everything ready for tomorrow morning?" she asked, looking around.

The doctor nodded. "Reverend Byington will conduct the service at ten, if that's all right with you." Patricia briefly smiled her assent.

"I'm grateful to you for arranging it all. I know so few people here."

"It's been my pleasure, my dear," he said.

"Doctor, may I ask you some rather unusual questions?"

"Certainly."

"Did you notice anything peculiar about my father's body when you prepared him for burial?"

"Yes, I did. I found physiological phenomena—things that were unusual."

"Like what?"

"I've never run in to anything like it." Patricia leaned forward, and the doctor continued, "If I had not known when he was killed, I would have said that his body was at least four days old. Now, I know that this doesn't jibe with the facts. There are certain diseases, such as diabetes, that cause abnormal changes in the tissues." He leaned back again. "Miss Laughlin, I tended your father several times, and I never found any indication of that disease. I'm at loss to explain the discrepancy."

"Could he have been dead for as much as a month?"

"I don't see how that could be. The body *was* abnormally rigid and the body fluids were . . . well, I just don't know."

"Thank you, Doctor. You've told me what you know. I've heard some strange things, and I just wanted your opinion. I'll see you tomorrow at the funeral."

***

Everyone left after Patricia's father was laid to rest. Patricia remained, desert flowers lingering in her hand. Her emotions seemed dried up. No tears had come. She wasn't going to wait for tears; the desire to get away from town pressed urgently on her. She stooped quickly to deposit the flowers on the grave.

As she leaned forward from the waist, she heard a waspish buzz and then the shot. She fell forward, parallel to the heap of newly turned soil. From this position she searched the brush on the edge of the cemetery for some sign of a hidden marksman. She saw no movement, not even powder smoke.

She lay on the ground for several minutes, afraid to move. She could feel her whole body quivering and clamped her teeth together to prevent them from chattering. Would life never be calm again? A nervous laugh pushed inside her as she considered her life might be over, here in the cemetery. She moved to her knees. There wasn't even a rustle of sage that she could detect. She scrambled, more slowly than she would have liked, toward the road, half expecting a bullet to crash into her back.

She gained the edge of town without mishap, then hurried passed shadowy alleys to the livery stable. She didn't take time to change back into her riding gear, but quickly set out on the road to the ranch.

The ranch house was empty—not even the cook was present. She drank a couple glasses of water, then went upstairs for her things. It must have been the quiet. She didn't know when she dozed off, but when she awakened it was dusk. There had been a sound downstairs. She slipped from her doorway to the top of the stairs.

There was a light in the living room. She hesitated and then saw that it was Bridger. He was pacing the floor with his hands behind his back as though in deep thought. He looked up and saw her.

"Come in, come sit down," he said. "I haven't had time to

talk to you since the funeral. Where did you go so early yesterday morning? I worried about you."

"I went for a ride."

"Well it's time we had a little talk about business. Have you made any plans?"

"I'll go back to San Francisco, I guess, after what happened today. Someone took a shot at me while I was alone in the cemetery." Bridger's eyes narrowed and his head turned a little.

"I know when I've been shot at."

"I suppose that's one way to get rid of you. With you and your father gone, it wouldn't be much of a trick to steal everything he worked so hard for."

"You mean you think one of Forester's crowd did it?"

"He killed your father, didn't he?"

"I'm not sure how my father died."

"Just what do you mean by that?"

"I saw Wade yesterday."

"Where? By heaven, I'd like to lay hands on him."

"I tried to shoot him back up on the mountain. I failed. He could have killed me quite easily right then. Why should he sneak down here and risk killing me where his enemies are?"

"He probably sent a dirty Indian to do the job."

"I don't think so, Bridger. But that's neither here nor there. I'm going to sell my holdings here, if I have any, and leave this country for good."

"But you . . . your father spent thousands of dollars and three years of his life on this land project."

"What do you suggest I do?"

"If you'll sign a power of attorney over to me, I'll see that his plan is completed."

"I'll have to think about it."

"Another way—a better way, I think—would be for you to marry me. As my wife, you'd have security. After we're married, you could take your trip to San Francisco—have yourself a good shopping spree. I could finish this project, and then we could live wherever you wished."

"It's a little too sudden. I just buried my father. I'm afraid I'd need a while to consider everything."

"Pat, I don't mean to be abrupt. But I've really given this a lot of thought. I told you, I'm in love with you. All this, it's your father's dream. He's kind of thrown us together by virtue of our lands and our mutual interests. You have a fine mind. I really need you to make this work. I need your companionship, your support. We can go far if we play it right. You'll have everything you've ever wanted."

Patricia's eyebrows raised. Bridger came toward her and ran his thumb down her arm. "We could go to Carson tomorrow. Please, Patricia. I wouldn't want to go on with this ranch—these plans—without you."

He pressed against her and kissed her. At first she responded, but there was no tenderness nor sincerity in his kiss. His actions reflected only desire. She moved away.

"I'm sorry, Bridger," she said. "I can't force this. If it comes at all, it must manifest itself as something I'm sure of. There was a time when your words might have swayed me. Marrying you at this point . . . just doesn't feel like what I want."

The expression on Bridger's face was tumultuous. He clearly struggled to keep some powerful emotion under control. "I suppose it's that yellow, loco drifter," he said thickly.

Patricia's face flamed in spite of her efforts at self-control. "That has absolutely no bearing whatsoever. You're being insulting. Every girl you meet isn't going to swoon in your arms just because you ask them to marry you. I think you presume entirely too much of such a short acquaintance."

His face softened, and the old, reckless look came over it. "I apologize. There's no fool like a jealous male. Well, I tried. If you're set on going, you can sign the necessary papers. I'll just keep you posted on developments."

"I see no need to sign anything right now."

"But certain documents have to be signed; certain decisions have to be made. I can't send a letter or telegram to the city every time I want to turn around."

Patricia was still a little piqued by Bridger's exhibition. "I'm sorry, but I'm not even sure that I want you handling my affairs."

She saw Bridger's neck redden. The flush rushed over his features like a tide. She was struck to the marrow with a sudden unknown fear. She caught a savage gleam in his eye as his hands snapped out and grasped her by the shoulders. His fingers dug in until she winced and quailed away, but he held her upright like a puppet.

XVII. Trapped

"**I**'m through fooling with you, you strumpet!" There was a deadly menace in Bridger's tone. "Those lonely nights in the hills with your friend Wade must have been quite a love feast. I've got news for you. Do you think I need you to carry out my plans? Your Uncle Pat signed over his third interest to me," he jabbed a finger at his chest. "That makes me two-thirds owner of everything. We're partners. Doesn't that make you happy?"

Patricia lifted her chin, here eyelids lowering. "Where is my uncle, anyway?" she said in a low tone. "Why would he sign everything to you and then disappear?"

"Oh, he's around. And just to make sure he doesn't squirm out of our deal, he's going to die—along with your beau, Forester. I'm not sure I won't kill you to make things less complicated. With you out of the way, the whole shebang is mine, get it? You thought you were going to run the show yourself, all high and mighty."

Patricia looked down. Threads of evidence began to fall into a pattern. Why did clarity have to come when she was alone, at Calhoun's mercy? Her eyes darted as Bridger's tirade became stage-worthy.

"Did you think you were dealing with one of those lily-white boys from the city? This is the raw west." His fingers relaxed, and his voice lowered. "If you marry me, I might let your uncle go. You're in no position to bargain, but you'll preserve what's left of your family—not to mention get a powerful husband in the deal."

Patricia suppressed a panicked urge to bolt. She pressed the warm suppleness of her body against Bridger. In her eyes was promise and surrender.

A smile replaced the brutish expression on Bridger's face as he looked down at her. "I knew you were the kind to appreciate a strong man with drive. As I said before, we'll make a wonderful tea—"

The sentence ended with sucked-in breath as Patricia turned like a trapped rat and bit into his hand. He wrenched his hand away, but before Patricia could get anywhere, he had her by the hair.

She reached for the mantle to keep from falling. Then her hand found the fire poker. As Bridger pulled her around, the poker came with her—and all her strength. She knocked him into a windowsill, where his scalp opened as he went to the floor. She lifted the poker again, but he swept her knees with his leg, and she collapsed. She tried to roll away, but he had a firm grip on her skirt. "You won't catch me off guard again," he spat.

She grasped the edge of a round library table and surged to her feet, leaving her skirt in his hands. She dove, sliding across the table on her stomach, knocking a huge, shaded kerosene lamp to the floor.

Bridger was up. He lunged at her again. She circled the table as he came around after her, like kids playing tag. Bridger was out of his head with fury. Blood ran down the side of his neck as he spat curses at her.

Patricia's back was to the wall when he gave the table a mighty heave, trying to pin her. She dodged, knocking a rifle off the wall. It fell between her legs and in front of her face—an easy grab—as she bounded across the room, with Bridger so close she could feel his breath. She felt his hand grasp her blouse. She jerked frantically, tearing loose. He lunged again, but she had time to topple a chair across his path. As he stumbled, she whirled and leveled the rifle.

The hammer fell on an empty chamber. She inwardly cursed, levering frantically enough to tip the barrel up as the gun exploded. The shattering boom in the closed room was earsplitting.

The slug tore through a curtain and bounced off the window frame. Gray, pungent powder smoke filled the room as Patricia worked the lever. Bridger stopped short like a reined-in cutting horse. But he was so berserk with rage that Patricia doubted the gun would save her. Bridger braced himself to dive forward as Patricia leveled and stared down the barrel at him, the waiting hammer eared back with the malevolence of a coiled rattler.

They faced each other with even eyes, air sucking noisily into their lungs. Patricia stood in a flimsy slip and a torn blouse. Bridger wiped his bloody, bitten hand across his sweaty forehead, leaving a crimson smear. In the dim light of a bracket lamp his face was a mask of wrath. "You'd better pull the trigger!"

"Come at me again and I'll oblige you."

"If you don't kill me now, you're done, that I guarantee!"

"We'll see."

"I mean it. I won't let an addlepated trollop like you stand between me and an empire."

"An empire won't fix your problem. Stand that table up and put your gun belt on it, slowly."

Bridger was gradually getting control of himself. He looked into Patricia's serious eyes, grudgingly righted the table, and laid the belted gun on it.

Patricia motioned him to stand back and then drew the heavy gun. She cocked it and laid the rifle on the table. Only when she let go of the rifle did her hand shake. "Now we'll see how you like a gun in your back. Turn around." Bridger faced away. "I'll be six feet behind you, so don't try anything—your empire wouldn't know what to do without you. Outside." When he was four feet from the door, Patricia said, "Stop. Lean forward until your hands rest against the door."

Patricia grabbed a coat off the wall, sliding one hand through the sleeve and throwing the other side of it over her other shoulder. Not bothering with the buttons, she gathered the collar with one hand and had Bridger open the door. "We're going to the tool shed—if you make it that far."

After having Bridger open the shed, she said, "Step inside, and I'll get out of your hair." Once Bridger was in, she dropped a bolt through the staple. She ran to the house for the rifle, decent clothes, and some food. In the corral she saddled her horse. As she rode out of the gate, she heard Bridger battering at the shed. She lifted the rifle and sent a slug through the top of the door. The noise stopped. She was soon out of the flatland and headed for the high country to the west.

XVIII. Pursued

Patricia stopped to breathe the horse at the edge of a meadow when a sound in a bush startled her. The moonlight through the branches enabled her to quickly spot the vicious creature causing the noise—a foraging porcupine. Farther on, she jumped when a roosting grouse exploded out of the brush at her elbow.

The air got nippier as she climbed into the mountain fastness. She had no idea what she was going to do. Her only thought was to get as far away from Bridger as possible. She knew she wouldn't make it out on the stagecoach. Several times, as she rested the horse, an impulse to turn back would ambush her. But there was no one in this country she could call a friend.

She rode up through Willow Flat and came at last to the cross trail that led to the lake. Her instinct was to keep moving west, in the hope that she could cross the Sierra Nevadas and make her way down into California.

She topped a high ridge and stopped to look back down the mountain. She caught occasional glimpses of campfires. The lower reaches of the range seemed to be dotted with men trying to trap Wade Forester. Now she too could be run into the ground like an animal. Once Bridger was free, she knew that these men would have orders to capture her—or perhaps shoot her on sight. She also knew that Wade's friends would make it hot for anyone who ventured too far into the mountains without the protection of numbers.

She lifted the reins and began to descend into a canyon. Near the bottom a sharp command came from a clump of brush above the trail. "Hold it and reach!" She obeyed and sat tensely as a form materialized out of the shadow and approached, gun drawn. "Who are you? Speak up!"

"Miss Laughlin . . . from the K-bar."

As her captor moved into view, Patricia recognized Luke Rafferty, one of Bridger's men. They called him High-Pockets—though some were starting to call him Lopsided Luke, since he'd recently lost an ear in a darkened saloon. "What are you doing up here?"

Patricia's heart hammered against her ribs. She could see herself being ignominiously dragged back to Bridger. Her thoughts were in turmoil as she tried to think of a plausible story that would account for her presence here. She decided that truth might serve. "You should know," she said boldly. "Someone tried to kill me yesterday."

"Is that so? Who?"

"How should I know? I only know that Mr. Calhoun is anxious to get rid of me. He seems to think I'm interfering with his plans."

"Yeah, I know. I seem to have heard something to that effect. But why over the mountain?"

"I don't trust him. I was afraid he might change his mind about letting me go and detain me if I tried to leave by stage."

"So what do you intend to do now?"

"I promised him I'd get out of his hair. That's exactly what I intend to do, if you'll let me." Patricia peered under the brim of his hat. "I've always had a lot of respect for you. You seem to be good with a gun. Isn't it dangerous for you to be so far up here with no backup? It must take a lot of courage," she added for good measure.

"We're trying to get a line on that Forester snake. He's pretty slippery. His Indian friends are on the prowl. Of course we got 'em outnumbered five to one, but they're still giving us trouble. I like you, Miss Laughlin. I s'pose I can let you pass since I haven't had any orders from Bridger to the contrary."

"I'll always remember your kindness. I'll really be very happy to get back to San Francisco."

Patricia left Rafferty and found the trail getting steeper as she climbed toward the pass. The dawn was just beginning to break when she saw a horseman riding down a side ridge toward the trail. She was coming up out of a canyon. As she topped the ridge, she recognized Wade astride his horse in the middle of the trail. As she pulled up, they eyed each other for several seconds.

"What are you doing back up here?" asked Wade with suspicion in his voice. "Thought you'd gone back to your friend at my ranch."

"I'm trying to leave the country," she repeated, more convinced with each recitation. "Had a little argument with Bridger."

"I've had you under my eye for the last half hour. I thought you were one of Bridger's men."

Pounding hooves exploded as a swarm of horsemen swept down onto the trail behind them.

"You've been setting a trap, you Delilah! I oughta shoot your . . ." Wade whirled his horse and spurred off up the trail.

Patricia's horse took off after Wade's. They smashed down

the canyon and charged up a quick rise. Across the canyon, shots popped and echoed toward them. Patricia flinched and sank low, as the firing seemed to urge her horse to more speed. Searching lead snapped and crackled through the brush and whined off of a silver-splashed rock.

Now she was absolutely tied with Wade in the minds of Bridger's men. There would be no convincing them otherwise.

Before she reached Wade at the top of the next ridge, he stopped and whirled his horse. To Patricia's horror, he whipped out his gun, pointing it in her direction. It belched flame and smoke and roared again. She ducked in terror, almost slipping from her horse. She couldn't turn back, and this madman barred her way with a death-spitting gun. But no bullets struck her. She realized he was firing over her head at the horsemen down the canyon.

The trail slid down to a bench, and the horses seemed to skim the earth as they fled. They ran at a stiff rise, grunting and scratching for traction. Then, with stiffened forelegs, they pegged their way to the bottom of a cutbank. Wade careened downhill onto the rough, trail-less mountainside.

Patricia's horse was eager, game, and fast, but Patricia marveled that either horse kept its feet. She had no time for fear; her muscles ached from squeezing against the barrel of the horse.

Now they were deep in the timber. Coming out, they headed for a clump of high brush. In the middle of this jumble of rocks and brush, Wade stopped. He squirmed out of his saddle, climbed or crawled over the top of the bush, and disappeared. Patricia could hear the men above calling back and forth to each other. He'd left her to the wolves! Though she found she could hardly blame him.

A ghostly voice blurted, "They're holed up in here somewhere. But they can't go no place from—"

Another sound cut in—an eerie, low clapping.

"There they go down the other side of the ridge!" said an excited voice. "How in tarnation did they get over there?"

Patricia heard the horsemen pull out and head toward the other side of the far ridge. A rustle and a scrape nearby made her start. Wade loomed up over the top of the brush. "That will take them off of our tail for a while," he said.

"What did you do?"

"An old Indian trick. I climbed to the top of the next ridge, found a large boulder, and rolled it down the canyon. It made plenty of racket. They'll be back, though. We'd better get out of here, pronto." Still, he paused. "You stick like a leech. What's the play?"

"No play. I told you, they want me as bad as they do you."

"Looks fishy. But I can't stop you from following me without tying you up—but now I'm reliving the past."

Patricia thought she caught a glint in his eye.

The horses stumbled and thrashed around until they were back in the timber where the ground was more receptive. Wade found a game trail and followed it upward. They lost themselves in a vast expanse of tall timber. When they came to a meadow, they skirted its edge. Just as they reached the other side, a shout went up behind them.

They lit onto a trail, the wind plucking at their clothing in its passing. At the bottom of steep canyons, creek beds leaped up at Patricia with the speed of her descent. Now it was dig and scratch to make the crest of the next ridge.

The riders behind them weren't gaining much, but they weren't losing sight of their quarry either. Wade reined off over a fairly open ridge. Rifles began to talk once more, and lead snatched at Patricia's saddle and bedroll. They headed toward a long mountain valley enclosed by sharp ridges and cliffs. The downgrade steepened, and the horses almost sat on their haunches as they negotiated the rough ground underfoot.

Suddenly Wade's horse did a complete forward roll. Wade

left the saddle, landing on hands and knees. He was up in an instant and swung up behind Patricia. A glance told him his horse had taken a slug in the paunch, but the heart and courage of the animal had kept it going for an additional hundred yards. Wade pointed. "In the canyon!"

Patricia peeled off of the ridge and the overloaded horse zigzagged its way down the canyon. The way out was unbelievably steep. The horse heaved and drove hard, but his two riders were too much for his tired muscles. Wade slid off, and Patricia followed. They scrambled up, leading the horse, and were nearly to the top of the ridge when rifle fire began to roll again.

They dove behind a rock. The horse screamed and reared over backward, tumbling into the canyon below. Wade said, "This is no good." He left the sanctuary of the rock in a sprinting run for the top of the ridge. Patricia followed as lead whipped divots from beneath their feet and left white splotches on nearby rocks.

Over and angling down into the next canyon, they heard curses behind them, and the sound of brush smashing, the scrabble of hard-ridden horses, and then a jubilant cry. "We got both horses! We'll have 'em on the hip."

The canyon was gorged with a matrix of thickly grown buck brush, stunted manzanita, and tall pungent weeds. Patricia and Wade scurried in like cover-seeking coyotes. Patricia was surprised to see that the growth was lusher than it appeared on the outside and laced with a variety of deer trails, rabbit, and other game paths. As they crawled in the tangle, thorny spines ripped their clothes and snagged Patricia's hair.

They worked their way down to the dry bed of a watercourse at the bottom of the canyon. After some distance they came to a small, level bench padded with dry grass. Here they paused to finally catch their breath. Sweat streamed down scratched faces as both their rib cages heaved from the exertion.

"This is it," said Wade resignedly. "The beginning of the end." Pointing, he said, "This canyon leads into that long valley. Once they drive us out into the open, we're finished."

"Thanks, but I'm already terrified." Patricia's expression went blank. "Still, I'd rather be dead than go back to the K-bar. Can they find us in here?"

"They're not ninnies. By now they know our rifles are on the saddles. They'll be closing in from all sides. If necessary, they'll set a torch to this pile of tinder and burn us out. It looks about hopeless. Well . . . guess I was crazy to think I could play hide and seek forever."

Seeing Patricia's panic turn to resignation, he said, "You'd better crawl out and see if they'll take you. Bridger will probably just put you on the stage and ship you out of the country."

"He won't do that now; I know too much."

"Then we'd better go on—as long as we can."

But Patricia grabbed Wade's arm. "What's that?"

Wade listened. There was a low rumbling, then they could feel the earth tremble. "Wild horses."

"Of course," said Patricia. "What next?"

"No, wait. All the shooting's frightened them. They're stampeding down the long valley. There must be several hundred of 'em. Come on!"

XIX. The Elements

They scurried down the dry watercourse. Where the mouth of the canyon emptied into the long valley there was a sharp cutbank about six feet high. They crawled out on this overhang and looked up the valley. A plume of dust trailed a great drove of horses as they poured down the valley. The awesome spectacle escaped Patricia, whose mind raced to understand what their next move was going to be.

Wade said, "They'll pass close to this ledge because the valley ends at this point. I think I can drop on a horse, ride out and—"

"Not without me!"

"You crazy? If you miss or get bucked off in that herd, you're mincemeat."

"I'll take any risk you will. At least I have a chance this way!" Then she added, "Uh, how do you stay on the back of a bucking wild horse?"

"They're not all wild; many have been lured away from domestic life by the wild ones. They'll swing right under us. They're too closely packed to buck very much." He mumbled, "I hope."

Patricia felt the tremor of the earth under her. If she failed to land on a horse's back, she'd be in the path of a thousand pounding hooves. She stilled her thoughts and hardened her resolve.

"All right," said Wade. "When they come under us, pick a mount that looks halfway tame. They may think we're mountain lions and use their teeth, so be careful. Grab a mane and hang on; even if you're dragged, don't let go." His gaze fixed somewhere on the right. "Ahh!" He pointed as the leaders thundered by. "See that black mare with the blaze face?" Now he was shouting. "She's going to have a colt soon; that'll slow her down. Those lighter patches on her side means she's been ridden. We'd better try to ride her double. If she tries to buck, there'll be too much weight and too little room. Ready?"

Patricia's head jerked quickly up and down.

"Get a good hold of my belt and drop when I do." The mare was on the inside of the drag and came loping in close to the outcropping. Wade crouched. As her head went by, he dropped. Patricia jumped with him, but the mare swerved away and banged into a nearby horse.

Patricia hit the rump of the mare and went over. Wade bounced belly-down across the withers but managed to sink his hand in the mane. The horse beyond the mare was a yearling colt. It had been crowded by the mare and could swerve no farther. Patricia still clung to Wade's belt, one leg over the mare's rump, her chest across the colt's back.

Wade finally got astride the mare. He reached back, grabbed Patricia by her riding skirt, and dragged her up onto the mare. Thundering along with the herd, the mare tried a few crowhops, but the weight of two riders quickly tired her.

After a run of nearly two miles, the herd began to settle down, finally turning up a side canyon. They continued up this for a half a mile and began to fan out. "Here's where we hit the dirt," said Wade. He helped Patricia drop first and then slipped

99

from the mare's back himself. The herd loped over a rise as stragglers caught up.

"Well, what now?" asked Patricia, breathing hard—more from the excitement than from exertion.

"We're safe from those human wolverines for a little while, but we're in tight." He looked around, then back to Patricia. "We've no horses, no weapons, no blankets, and no food. We can't go down into the open. Looks like we have to head for the big divide and cross into the Mother Lode Country. It'll be tough," he said, his eyes searching for a route. "The saddle is eleven thousand feet high. And, uh, I hate to tell you this, but those thunderclouds could bring snow at this altitude. It looks like there's nothing for us but to take the risk."

Patricia sat where she was. Wade crouched next to her. "We can only rest for about an hour," he said. "And then we've got to start over the top."

"Good," said Patricia. Wade stared at her. "After that last ride, I think I'd prefer a hike."

"That bareback riding and leaping shake you up a little?"

"I was riding the part that went the highest, remember? I keep thinking of where I'd be if I hadn't been able to hang on to your belt."

Wade put a blade of grass in his mouth. "I used to curse those broomtails, but they sure came in handy when the chips were down. I won't begrudge the few mares I lost to those marauding stallions after this."

Patricia turned and looked up to the tops of the craggy peaks to the west. They were slashed by streaks of snow and ice that lay in the crevices of their deep canyons. The air was so clear that it seemed they couldn't be more than a mile or so beyond the nearest ridge. She was soon to find out just how far those close-appearing peaks were.

They began a slanting climb toward a low saddle south of a peak. The sky to the north began to frown with a threatening mass of dark clouds that usually presages a mountain storm. In an hour it hit them with a slashing gale. They rested for a moment in the hollow of a dead tree. Wade would look at her and then look at the ground. Perhaps he wouldn't meet her gaze because she was studying him so intently. They set out again.

Late in the afternoon, Patricia's stomach started complaining. She had not eaten all day, and the cold and exertion were rapidly depleting her energy.

A stygian darkness wrapped the mountain in a mantle that defied the eye to pierce it. Then the heavens themselves seemed to open. The torrent drove against them behind a wind that was a near hurricane. Limbs tore from surrounding trees and went crashing into the canyons. Trees bowed and curtsied. Leaves turned their undersides to show a lighter green.

Wade and Patricia slogged on. Wade managed to keep to a game trail they had been following. There was no cover, no respite from the biting wind.

Patricia heard a whistling roar and a crash followed by an earth-quaking shock. She cried out against the wind, "What was that?"

"We just missed being hit by a falling tree. That pine must have been five feet through."

As quickly as it began, the rain and wind ceased. They ran into a tangle of limbs and tree trunks where two forest giants had gone down across the trail. There was nothing to do but feel their way through this matrix and hope they would not miss the trail on the other side.

The temperature dropped. Something soft caressed Patricia's face. The third time this happened, she realized it was snowing. In half an hour they were moving like ghosts through a snowstorm.

Wade tied his bandanna to his belt, and Patricia grasped the knotted end to keep from losing him in the dark. They plodded on wordlessly through a white world they could sense more than see. The only sound was the squeak of the snow under their feet.

Patricia became so fatigued she seemed to be walking in a semi-coma, hardly conscious of putting one foot in front of the other. Her damp riding skirt began to stiffen as the cold struck it. She had tripped and fallen so many times that she lost track. Always, Wade helped her to her feet without a word and plodded on up the steep trail.

Patricia now applied all the force of her will to move. Her mind fatigued at the simple task of keeping her legs in motion. She could feel herself slowing Wade as he half drug her along. Her feet were so cold that a twinge of pain shot up her legs whenever she put her weight on them. She finally stopped and said, "I'm done. I simply can't go on."

"It's death to stop now," said Wade. "You've got to keep going."

"I can't. Can't."

Wade stepped back and hooked an elbow under her armpit and propelled her forward. Patricia felt a little irked, and she wondered where he got the strength to keep going, much less drag her along. She was completely dazed until they both fell over some impediment in the trail. Wade got up, but Patricia lay in the snow. It was such a heavenly feeling, just to lie there. A beautiful sensation of warmth flooded over her. She felt so relaxed. She wanted very much to go to sleep.

Wade felt for her in the dark, grabbed her by the hand, and tried to get her up. She mumbled, "Let me be. I'm fine. Please let me rest."

Wade said savagely, "You little fool. You're half frozen— that's why you feel warm. If you lie here, you'll be dead in an hour. Get up!"

He picked her up by the armpits, but she slumped back to the snow. Her body just wouldn't respond to her will. In fact, she had no will. All she wanted was for blissful oblivion to overtake her. She was vaguely conscious that Wade was down beside her in the snow.

Then he hit her. Hard.

Her arms raised defensively in panic as he struck her again across the face. The pain was ten times what it would have been because her nerves were raw from the cold. Patricia rolled her body away from Wade, but he was over her again. She grabbed his frozen ears.

Crying out in pain, Wade pulled her to her feet, then said roughly, "That's better. If you can fight a little, you can walk. Now move."

He propelled her forward once more, and she staggered and weaved in his grip. It wasn't long before she had a sensation of floating—a jarring kind of levitation—and her short snatches of consciousness told her she was being carried.

It was a fitful sleep. Patricia could feel Wade's whole body shake from the fatigue that must be in his every muscle. She felt him stagger and fall, but she couldn't even extend a limb to break her own impact.

The snow stopped. There was a pungent odor of sulfur in the air. Patricia felt Wade stir himself to his feet again. In Wade's arms she had felt rest. But she sensed she was alone now.

Not really opening her eyes, she perceived a hint of light. The night was ending.

Wade stood over her again. "Come on," he said to no one able to hear. He dragged her a short distance by her arms, then managed somehow to pick her up one last time. Patricia forced her eyes open, but saw only a misty fog. The cold returned savagely; her body was one complete ache.

She felt Wade drop her, and quickly knew she was over a precipice. She could not scream, but felt resigned to a sudden, unexpected end. So Wade had finally decided to rid himself of her forever.

XX. The Devil's Kitchen

Midair, Patricia involuntarily braced her body and mind against the shock of striking a bed of sharp rocks. The impact knocked the wind out of her. But she did not anticipate the splash, and water closing over her head. She was sinking. She flailed with her arms and kicked. As she broke the surface, her intake of air was interrupted by the concussion of Wade's body hitting the water beside her.

Wade soon bobbed to the surface. Being tossed over a ledge had been such a shock that it was only now she realized she was treading warm water. Wade grabbed her by the jacket and began swimming on his side. She kicked her feet to assist his progress.

They only had to move about five yards to a shallow section of the hot pool. Wade lay on his back and rested his head on the bank—completely exhausted—with most of his body floating in the pool. Patricia rested her head against one of his arms and, in seconds, was sound asleep.

Several hours later, Patricia finally opened her eyes. She looked everywhere at once. She was lying on the edge of a pool at the foot of a yellowish bluff. What she had dreamed to be a nice hot bath was actually a hot sulfur spring. She could hear the runoff as water slid out between the banks of a chrome-yellow gully into the brush below.

She glanced at Wade as he lay with his head pillowed on his arm. His breathing was stentorious. His face, covered with black stubble, was still drawn with fatigue. Lines of weariness pulled at his eye corners, and his bruised cheeks were sunken and hollow. He must have carried her for miles up the steep trail. She blew out a deep breath. She felt very secure. She liked being this close to Wade.

A movement animated the corner of her vision. She turned her head slowly. Her eyes finally focused on a sight that would forever be impressed on her memory. It sucked her breath in and froze her like stone. For a few seconds, she wanted her senses to refuse to record it, to deny its existence. The thing before her was enormous and capable of flicking out a life with one twitch of its gigantic strength.

She beheld an adult male grizzly bear. The great, gray chest was toward her. Its sides were matted with yellow mud, and dirty water streamed from his coat to the ground. It was about ten yards away and had just emerged from one of the hot pools. It stood, doglike, and raised an inquisitive muzzle to keen the air.

Suddenly, it reared up to its total height and spread its great claws. In this position, its stature was beyond intimidating. The claws were an ivory yellow and six inches long. The flared nostrils were as big as half dollars. The head was broad and massive.

It dropped to all fours, and the inquisitive snout snuffed at the ground, showing the long, silvery hair of its neck and back. Patricia poked Wade's ribs surreptitiously under the water. His eyes came open with full awareness. She rolled her eyes in the direction of the bear. He glanced that way just as the bruin began an ambling, swinging walk directly toward them. Wade covered Patricia's nose and mouth with a calloused hand, and together they slowly sank out of sight in the depths of the pool. After what seemed an eternity for Patricia, her lungs began to burn with the desire for air. Her diaphragm sucked downward spasmodically, but Wade's hands held her fast.

When it seemed she would black out from suffocation, Wade brought her slowly to the surface. With eyes and noses barely protruding, they looked cautiously around. Directly in front of them on the far edge of the pool were the bear's hindquarters. It had stopped and seemed to be gazing into the brush beyond. It was so close that a long stick would have reached its muddy sides. It turned. To Patricia, the bulking sides had the mass of a boxcar. It blew out a snort of air, nibbled at some thorn between its paws, and then made its way down the little watercourse below the spring.

After the treading of paws and claws dissipated, Wade let out a breath.

"Wooh! That was close," he said barely audibly. "I'm not in the mood to share a bath with a grizzly."

"Would he have attacked us?"

"Possibly not. This sulfur smell is pretty strong, and being under water covered most of our smell. But those beasts are unpredictable. If it had seen us, there's no telling what it would have done."

"Runty little thing, wasn't he?"

Wade grinned. "I've shot a couple, and you can take my word for it: You'll never see a bigger one. They come to wallow in the hot mud." He stretched. "I didn't think we'd make it here. When I got to the edge of the pool, I didn't have the strength to set you down like a lady. I just dropped you and fell in after you."

"I only remember thinking I'd died and the Devil was casting me into hell's cauldron. I never knew a hot bath could feel so good." Patricia dared to move her upper body to the soil. She removed her boots. "What's that hissing sound?"

"This is volcano country. Hot rocks are just below the surface. That sound is a spring running over the heated granite. The water turns to steam and the pressure causes it to hiss through the cracks." Still sitting in the water, he asked, "How do you feel?"

"A hundred years old," said Patricia, rubbing her feet. "My muscles feel like someone beat me with a club. I keep hearing bullets hitting the ground or the roar of stampeding hooves. I've just been scared out of half of my growth, and I'm so hungry—it's a good thing that bear got out of sight."

"Maybe I can find some game before you decide to eat me." Wade climbed out of the pool and helped Patricia sit on the bank. She looked about and saw a great barren swath. The whole area was denuded of trees or soil of any kind, revealing the grayish granite. A twenty acre section of the mountainside had been blown away by some terrific, subterranean explosion.

Clouds of steam hissed into the air from several clefts in the rock. Around the periphery of this bare expanse lay a foot or more of newly fallen snow. It had attacked this bastion, but the heat had melted it, kept it at bay. A creek that ran in and out of the spot had ice on its banks above and below the volcanic area. Patricia was seeing things she dimly remembered reading about, but the actuality was a source of great wonderment to her.

Wade said, "Just rest up here. I'll be back."

"Do you think he'll return?" Patricia said, a little hesitantly.

"I hardly think so. Just stay near pool and, if he should come back, play turtle again." She thought she saw him wink.

Wade returned in about an hour with a great, bluish mountain hare. As he took out his knife, Patricia stood and walked to where she could feel heat emanating from the granite. "Fine. And what do we do—eat it raw?"

"Don't sell raw meat short. It's real good when you're hungry."

"Ugh!"

"I have no dry matches, and if I did, there's hardly anything around here dry enough to burn. Besides, a cooking fire would only advertise our location."

"I don't think I'm quite that hungry."

"Oh, well, time will take care of that. I'll eat this one and, when your hunger overcomes your squeamishness, I'll shoot another one, although getting close enough to shoot one with a Colt is quite a trick."

"Where *is* the next restaurant?"

"About fifty miles or so over the roughest country in the Sierras."

Wade positioned the knife and, with a few deft strokes and a couple of jerks, skinned the animal then gutted it. He held the naked flesh out to Patricia. "Sure you don't want any?"

Patricia recoiled, but her salivary glands began to work.

Wade laughed. "I was only having a little joke. Watch closely while the great chef shows you how a hare is done to a turn."

Wade's laugh startled Patricia. She had always seen him dour and grim of visage. For a moment, it was like meeting a stranger.

He cut a long pole that was sticking out of a snowbank and whittled it sharp with the knife. He pierced the rabbit at one end, and then the sharp point of the pole exited the other. He walked over to a crevice that was exuding steam. He held it in the steam for about ten minutes. When it was withdrawn, it was thoroughly cooked.

He tore a leg off and handed it to Patricia. She set her teeth into it rather gingerly. Soon she was blissfully chewing, and Wade smiled at her expression of ecstasy. Her eyes twinkled as she mumbled between bites, "How stupid can a person get? Here we are in the middle of the Devil's kitchen, and I'm worried about how to cook him!"

They cleaned the rabbit down to the bones, and Wade said, "We can't stay here. We've got a tough day ahead; we need to get over that pass. It will be nip and tuck all the way—especially without food. Just have to keep moving. How do you feel?"

"Wonderful. I could eat another one, but I feel stronger." Sitting by the hot rocks had dried their clothes, but it was still chilly.

"Good. Here we go again," said Wade.

By late afternoon, they approached the foot of the pass. Patricia's pace slowed again. Fortunately, the temperature had risen, but the wind that came off of the peaks was knifelike when it blew. Because of the altitude Patricia could only progress a few hundred yards without stopping to rest. Her heart raced until she thought it would jump out of her chest. The back of her hands felt prickly, and there was a buzzing, vibratory sensation in her limbs.

But a few minutes rest would make her feel like going on again. They topped a sharp rise and looked down into a little bowl-shaped valley. As their heads loomed over the crest, Wade threw out his arm and stopped Patricia. He pointed up toward the head of the little valley.

For a moment Patricia saw little to excite her imagination. Now, as her eyes focused, she saw a sight that is only given to a privileged few. Before her were nine or ten mountain sheep. These graceful, wild things were nonchalantly grazing, and seemed oblivious to the presence of humans.

Two fine bucks with massive, curving horns stood guard on pinnacles. They were as immobile as statues against the background of lofty peaks. Patricia stood, enthralled. In a flash the whole band was in mad flight, nimbly executing impossible leaps as they skimmed across the face of a seemingly sheer cliff. In seconds they were gone from sight.

"There goes the very soul of the high country," said Wade solemnly. "Those bighorns live in the very clouds—independent of every other creature."

Patricia gave him a curious glance. Any kind of sentiment seemed foreign in her companion, this man with whom she had covered so much rough territory.

Now they approached a great plain of utter devastation. Massive slabs of granite as big as houses formed grotesque patterns, caves, and shadows. They threaded their way through this maze and finally reached the smooth, wind-scrubbed area below the pass. Here an icy gale struck them head-on. They leaned into its force as they struggled upward. They paused to rest in the lee of an overhang and looked back over the way they had come.

Below them was the fringe of stunted trees at the timberline. Stretching toward the horizon were the undulating folds of timbered ridges that charged down to the yellow floor of the vast desert. Out of this floor, naked buttes reared their bald heads skyward. Dry lakes and patches of salt and alkali glittered in the distance. Patricia was awed by the sweep and majesty of these vast worlds. Her lungs tingled and stung from breathing the rarefied air.

They climbed again. Patricia wondered if they would ever reach the top of the divide. With Wade's help she finally got to the crest. Here they rested again and looked to the west. As far as the eye could see were the timbered slopes of the Sierras, bathed in a rose and gold aura as the setting sun touched the clouds and the far haze over this open sanctuary.

The downhill going was easier and they made timberline before dark. Patricia was on the verge of complete exhaustion as the night closed in. After an interminable interlude of walking in a daze, Patricia heard Wade say, "Here we are."

Patricia was dimly aware that they had entered some sort of a shelter. She sensed the press of piney needles under her feet, and her nostrils were assailed by a pleasant, woody smell that she could not clearly analyze. She sank and lay on a bed of resilient needles. High above her, she could faintly see a star filtering its meager light down to her. The rest was blackness. As she dropped off into an exhausted slumber, she entertained the quaint idea that she was sleeping in a tepee and that the starlight was drifting down through the usual hole in the top.

Her senses came back to her slowly, and she was conscious of that mysterious, pleasant odor. She finally opened her eyes and glanced idly about. She was surrounded on all sides by charred, blackened walls that leaned in on her and seemed to meet in a peak above her. She saw a round patch of blue sky directly over her. The opening was at least two hundred feet above her head. Her shelter was mostly a half gloomy darkness. Before her, she could make out a V-shaped opening as tall as a man.

Wade was nowhere to be seen. Her surroundings puzzled her; she arose and walked out through the narrow opening. With an eerie feeling, she examined the place where she had spent the night. Her bedroom was a cavity in the base of a huge fire-gutted tree.

And such a tree! It was at least twenty feet in diameter where its flared butt drove its supporting roots into the earth. The fire had not only hollowed out the base but had ranged upward until the tree was a live chimney. As she continued to examine her surroundings, she was overcome with reverent awe.

She stood in a little amphitheater of level ground and was completely surrounded by huge trees that flung their heights into the vastness of the sky. These trees had rough, thick bark with a reddish cast. She had heard of these trees, but this was her first look at the gigantic Sequoia redwoods.

The sunlight filtered down to her like golden lances of soft light. Dispersed through the trees were great, palm-like ferns that sprayed upward to a height of seven or eight feet. The undersides of the leaves were embroidered with golden spores.

The glade seemed a cathedral, with the huge boles of the trees rearing themselves up, like spires, toward the heavens.

At the base of her tree tepee, Patricia found a pile of fragrant needles. Her stomach was a gnawing ache of hunger. She sat against the tree and, in the warmth of a late autumn sun, closed her eyes. When she had occasion to open them again, she found herself gazing into the yellow eyes of a huge mountain lion. It was about twenty feet away and stood broadside to her. Its long tail moved lazily from side to side. It appeared to be looking directly at or beyond her. It half squatted and began to shuffle the needles with its hind feet.

Patricia felt for the entrance to the tree. If she could get back inside, perhaps she could block the opening with a fallen branch.

Before she could move it sprang with effortless speed and vanished from sight. Patricia was surprised to hear her breath expelled with an audible sigh of wonder. She hadn't had time to become terrified.

But she didn't want to stay out in the open anymore. Once she was sure she had a large enough tree limb, she retreated to her sanctuary, blocked the opening, and waited for Wade's return.

She dozed again. And then some dim, faraway sound drifted into her unconscious state and roused her from what seemed a drugged sleep.

As she came awake, it took her seconds to orient herself. There was movement outside her wooden fortress and a surreptitious sound—the padding of animal feet. She peeked out through slits in the entrance and saw a dark brown patch of hair within inches of her face. She recoiled with a slight shriek of fear. The animal let out a horrible bellow that prickled her scalp. Now fully awake, she quickly realized that what she thought might be a ferocious animal was a huge hound.

XXI. Resolve

He bayed again, and another dog ran into sight. They circled the hollow tree, yelping and howling (like hound dogs) as though threatening to attack without further ado. When Patricia began to doubt the security of the entrance, she heard a shrill whistle, and the dogs dropped to the ground. They lay with tongues hanging out of the sides of their capacious muzzles.

A lanky figure entered the clearing. A stubble of iron-gray beard covered a long, grim face. He strode to her fortress and said, without any ceremony or attempt at an introduction, "Get your pins under you; we's goin' to my camp."

When Patricia started to demure, he said, "Wade's sent me. He's rid my cayuse down to get some horses."

He turned abruptly and set off down the trail, the hounds ranging in front of him. His stride was a shambling, slack-kneed gait that kept Patricia at a trot to keep up with him. In about twenty minutes they arrived at a large, sun-drenched clearing.

"This is her," he announced dryly.

On the far side of the clearing was a gigantic tree that dwarfed any she had yet seen. It seemed buttressed by a splay of root shanks that swept upward to form the main bole of the tree. Great gnarled burrs, round and big as washtubs, stuck out from the trunk. They were rough and irregular—like huge warts.

Most amazing was the fact that this burled, twisted monarch was being utilized as a human habitation. The door was made of crude planks split from redwood timber. On each side of the door were openings to let light in. A blackened, tin stovepipe jutted out from the side, a thin column of grayish smoke drifting up from this flue. On the left of this tree house was a huge log. It was about ten feet high. The sides were covered with a thick, green moss, and several ferns sprouted from the top.

Patricia caught a movement on top of the log. A sad, bearded but wise face looked down at her. The drawn face belonged to a goat. He was quite a specimen. Long, white-and-brown fleecy hair covered his neck, chest, and forelegs. His body was covered with short hair, but the hindquarters were clothed in a long fleece that gave him the ludicrous appearance of wearing chaps. Two black, shiny horns twisted and spiraled upward for nearly two feet.

The goat leaped gracefully off its high perch and dropped the ten feet to the ground. Without hesitation, it charged Patricia. She shrank behind the tall man. The goat stopped in front of him, butted gently against his thigh, and stepped back expectantly. The man reached into the pocket of his greasy, black buckskins and pulled out a chunk of chewing tobacco. He tore off a huge piece. The goat took it from his hand and walked away, chewing contentedly. The man said, "I'm Milo. This here critter's called Moses."

They continued across the clearing toward the tree house, and again Patricia was startled by a scene she couldn't initially grasp. Some four or five objects came hurtling toward her like leaves borne on the wind. She soon realized that they were flying squirrels. They swooped down, banked gracefully, and alighted on the trapper as light as thistledown. She glanced upward just as another took off from a limb two hundred feet from the ground. It volplaned downward at terrific speed, tipped its webbed body upward, and came to rest on the goat's back.

Patricia felt a light, feathery touch on her thigh. She looked down to find a squirrel clinging to her skirt. At first it gave her a start. The furry animal climbed up to her shoulder and then rested for a second at the base of her neck. Then it was gone as it leaped to the shoulder of the trapper, who gave it a pine nut.

Milo stooped by the tree house entrance and handed Patricia a ladle with spring water in it. It was cold and sweet, and she quickly downed it.

They entered the house. Ax and adze had been used to chop away a charred interior. This exposed the deep, red grain of the wood, which had been coated with something that gave it a glossy sheen. There was a burled, bull's-eye effect. Split redwood boards formed the floor. The trapper motioned her to a homemade chair with a buckskin seat. Patricia's stomach was contracting as her nose smelled the odors of food. She was so ravenous she was tempted to leap to her feet and try to find some morsel to chew on.

Milo busied himself at the stove. In a matter of minutes he set a great platter of food on a table and motioned her to the board. The aroma made Patricia dizzy. Three beautiful fried eggs rimmed a slab of ham half an inch thick. Milo reached into the oven and brought out several fragrant sourdough biscuits. Before Patricia was a jar of blackish wild honey, a plate of butter, and a pitcher of goat cream.

Patricia's eyes widened as a plate of sliced tomatoes appeared. "Where did you get these?" she asked blissfully.

"I growed 'em. Where do you think I got 'em?"

In twenty minutes Patricia was stuffed—sated until she

couldn't swallow another bite. She took the dishes to a redwood sideboard, then went outside for another drought of the heavenly spring water.

Wade had returned. He and Milo stood talking by some horses as she approached. Wade acknowledged her with a nod, pausing long enough to say, "Milo Snyder, this is Miss Laughlin."

The old trapper grunted an acknowledgment and said to Wade, "So you fit Bridger's boys and got whupped. What now?"

"I don't know," said Wade. "All I can do is wait and keep my eyes open for a break. Bridger has fifty men—quite a payroll. There are certain things they just can't do until I'm out of the way. As long as I'm alive, I'm a monkey wrench in the machinery."

"Sure, sure. But you ain't got no charmed life. It only takes one bullet."

"What else can I do, stroll into court and file a suit for my rights? One of the Laughlin brothers is dead and the other can't be found. I can't start legal proceedings against the Laughlins until Patricia's uncle turns up. With the courts and judges favorable to Bridger, the litigation could go on for years."

Patricia spoke up. "Just what is this suit about that might be brought against me?"

"Well," said Wade, "your uncle's land company has a shady title to the K-bar. I can prove, in a fair court, that half of the K-bar is mine. Without that ranch, whatever plans are afoot can be stopped. The present title can be established, should I be found dead, because Bridger is the husband of my sister. Bridger's also got to get you out of the way—or divorce my sister and convince you to marry him."

"That was made clear to me, achingly," said Patricia, hands to her temples.

"But he won't file papers until I'm six feet under, otherwise, a divorce weakens his claim to the K-bar. On the other hand, if the K-bar remains in my hands, you lose. All the titles and options on land in the valley are of little value without the K-bar. Every dime you might inherit is tied up in this. If it goes bust—and I intend to see that it does—you end up with nothing. You might still have some land of your father's, but no cash to manage it. Worst of all, you'd have little likelihood of finding a buyer, since the main water and other rights that give it any value are attached to my property."

Patricia bristled a little. "If I have any rights—and I expect to find out what they are—I'll fight for them. I know that the land company holds title to several thousand acres that are mine and Uncle Pat's. We'll fight for what is ours."

"I expect you to . . . if you live." Wade slowed and softened his tone. "This thing is so big. Bridger won't stop at murder to get his way. He has the power, and the men, to see his plan through."

"What are you going to do?" Patricia asked.

"I'm going back over the divide. I don't think you'll want to risk your life again."

"I . . . haven't had a chance to thank you," she said.

"What happened was practically thrust on us; past is past. My advice to you is to go where it's safe and lie low until this blows over and you know where you stand. Milo will take you to Sonora. From there, you can get a stage to San Francisco."

Wade struck Milo's hand. "I surely appreciate all your help, my friend."

"Warn't nuthin'," Milo returned.

Wade paused. He gave a quick nod to Patricia, mounted up, and was off again. Patricia watched him lope off through the trees and was suddenly awash in a feeling all too familiar to her—abandonment. Never mind that she had been shot at, kidnapped, wrestled, starved, pursued, nearly frozen, and dragged along until she was beyond the point of complete exhaustion; this thing went farther back—and deeper. It had been freshly ripped open again with the death of her father.

"If we's gonna make Sonora today, we better get started," Milo said, as kindly as his gruff voice would let him.

Patricia put her head down and tried to focus on the present. If she returned from beyond the divide, she faced the prospect of being killed. She should, logically, go to the safety of civilization and wait for developments, but she had a stake in those developments.

"Wait. Wait," she said to herself, then mumbled, "What have I got to wait for?"

Patricia looked at Milo and her bewildered, lost look began to change into another expression. The muscles at the corner of her jaw bunched as she peered into Milo's countenance. Somehow, she was going to get what was rightfully hers. "Could you loan me a horse, blankets, and some food?"

"Sure," said Milo, scratching his head. "I got a slab of bacon, some flapjack flour, and some airtights. Reckon I can spare a couple of blankets."

XXII. Flight

Patricia rode north, following Wade's trail. His horse's tracks were plain enough in the wet soil. She urged her mount along and hoped to catch Wade before he crossed over the eastern slopes. But she dropped into the timberline on the other side and still hadn't spotted him.

She roweled her horse to greater speed. Coming around a turn in the brushy section of the trail, she was startled by a sudden movement in front of her. A huge mule tail buck was charging her position. Something had disturbed it, and now it was running at full speed. It slid to a stop, whirled in its tracks, laid a great rack of horns back along its shoulders and scampered back the way it had come. Patricia's horse charged after it in apparent glee, and they raced down the trail until the buck found a convenient spot to turn off into the brush.

***

Not far ahead of her, Wade rode toward the chief's ranch. A thought had come to him that made him want to hurry. It was the kind of idea that he kicked himself for not considering before. Why hadn't he realized that his sister's life might be in danger?

He was so engrossed with his thoughts that he became careless. He rode over the top of a ridge and saw a group of horsemen just as they saw him. His horse wasn't too fresh, but he hooked in the spurs and dashed back the way he had come.

The ridges were mostly buckbrush and sage at this point, offering little cover. By the time he reached the crest of the next ridge, he knew that the fresher horses would soon overtake him. He would be forced back into more open country where other riders might join in the chase. He had a better chance if he could get to the timber of the lower country.

Crossing a small open flat, he decided that desperate measures were in order. Beyond this flat was a rolling hump of ground. He rode over this section of the trail and dropped from the sight of Bridger's men. He peeled the borrowed rifle from its boot and whirled his horse, dashing back up over the rise in a spurt of gravel. Wade smashed into his pursuers with the lever of the rifle working madly. A horse reared in fright as Wade's horse struck it; both horse and rider went down.

Guns exploded almost in Wade's face. The rifle ran dry, and he laid about him with the heavy barrel. Two more men were out of the saddle besides the man that had gone over with his horse.

The remaining rider was trying to bring his mount under control for a shot. Wade's horse reared and spun at the same time Wade's Colt .45 came up. He missed the first shot, then felt his horse shudder as it took a slug somewhere in the body. His second shot knocked the last man out of the saddle.

One of the unhorsed men was on his feet, and Wade cut down on him with leveled gun. He held his fire when he saw that the rider was hard hit and out of the fight. Wade spun his horse and fled back down the trail. He felt lucky and quite thankful that he had smashed his way through. He went twenty yards when his horse suddenly piled up and threw him hard to the earth.

The rider that had gone down with the horse in the first rush was up and leveling a gun. Wade drew and thumbed the hammer, but it fell on a spent shell. A bullet kicked up dirt at his feet. The rider sensed Wade's predicament and set himself for a finer aim. Wade dove behind the downed horse. He shucked shells out of his belt and reloaded his gun as an occasional slug tore viciously into the dead animal.

Wade was trapped. In minutes the gunshots would bring reinforcements swooping into the fray. His spent rifle was in the boot with the full weight of the horse on the scabbard. He was frantic. The next gunshot was rifle talk. He knew that to expose himself to such close-range fire would be fatal.

The drum of a fast running horse vibrated the ground beneath him. He barely squinted over the barrel of the horse to see how many riders were closing in. A new rider swept over the crest of the ridge and bore down toward his position. Wade's prognostication was that he was outgunned and outflanked.

He gathered himself for a last, desperate sprint to the dubious cover of a brush patch ten yards away. The firing had stopped, so he risked another quick look.

The approaching horseman came pounding on. The man with the Winchester half rose from his prone position behind a horse and tried to dodge to one side just as the rider's horse hit him and knocked him sprawling. His rifle flew out of his hands, and he rolled over and over from the impact.

The horse hardly changed stride as it leaped over the dead animal and headed straight for Wade's fleshy breastworks. Wade laid his gun barrel over the rounded belly of the horse and tried to get a bead on the rider who was low behind the horse's neck.

He let the hammer fall but tipped the barrel up just as he saw that the rider was Patricia.

The horses forelegs pegged to a slower speed, and Wade sprang to a seat behind the cantle. He wanted to wrap his arms around Patricia, but she shouted, "What's this? I try to rescue you and almost get my head blown off!"

"My mistake. How was I to know you were still in the country? I thought you were headed to Sonora."

"Are you sorry I changed my mind?"

"Lordy, no. You were Johnny-on-the-spot!" His voice was filled with admiration.

"I heard the shots, so I rode down to see if I could help."

"You helped all right. They would've had me salted away in another ten minutes. I owe you."

"Don't mention it. Maybe that helps to even our little score." She looked around. "Where to now?"

Wade nodded ahead. "Follow the trail. They'll be on our tail in a few minutes. I'm sure the woods are full of 'em. We'll have to shake them again—and it'll take more than wild horses this time. If we can lose them, we'll need to hide out until things quiet down. I think I know a place we can try for."

"No more snowcapped peaks and grizzly bears, please!"

"This . . . may be worse."

"Why didn't I take that nice long stage ride? I'm getting tired of being pursued like a fox."

"So now you know what my life is like," said Wade, smiling behind her. Then, in mock judgment, he added, "You had a choice. What did you expect when you came back to this country, a tea party?"

"Of course," Patricia smiled. "I'll stop the complaints. What could be worse than what I've already gone through? I'm still kicking, somehow. Bring on the trial by torture," she said with a smirk.

The horse covered several miles with its double burden, and

its wet sides heaved. Patricia pulled it down to a walk to give it a break.

They entered the gloom of a stand of firs and tamarack. They proceeded for a mile into this forest when Wade said, "Pull up. This is it."

Patricia stopped the horse and looked around. She saw nothing to be stopping for. They were under the spreading limbs of an enormous fir tree, but there was no sign of a place to hide.

Wade said, "I hope you brought some food with you."

"You picked a fine time for a picnic. You planning to invite Bridger's men to this meal?"

"You'll need some energy, that's all."

"I brought bacon, canned beans, and some of Milo's biscuits."

"Good. Dismount on those pine needles and don't move. Here, hold the blanket roll. The food's inside, I hope?"

Patricia nodded.

"I'll be back shortly. I'm going to ride down the trail, throw the saddle into a canyon, and turn the horse loose. That should throw them off for a little while."

"Again?" asked Patricia. "No horse, no rifle, and no place to go—thank heaven for blankets and food!" Wade started off. "Wait. How do we get away from here, fly into the blue?"

"You may take to the air before we're through. Hang tight; I'll be right back."

Patricia stood holding the bedroll, utterly confused. She kept an apprehensive eye on the back trail. She would not have been surprised to see riders sweep down on her. A voice behind her said, "Ready?"

Patricia recognized Wade's voice, but it startled her. As she turned, he handed her a pair of gloves.

"What now?" she asked, thoroughly confused.

"You'll need these. That crack about flying wasn't far off!"

Wade grinned, but it didn't make her feel any better. "We're trying to get to a place called Diamond Mesa. Unfortunately, the trail between here and there is a regular highway for Bridger's men.

Wade draped the food-laden blanket roll over his shoulders and dropped the coils of a lasso rope over his head. He reached up and grasped a low-hanging limb of the huge tree and pulled himself up into the branches. Patricia took a breath, let her shoulders fall, and said, "Here I come."

She scrambled up on to the overhanging limb.

Wade stood up on the limb, grabbed the limb above it for balance, and made his way to the trunk of the tree. Patricia followed.

They drew themselves higher and higher. The trees were so close together they were able to proceed out on one limb and cross over to an adjacent tree. "I used to play in trees when I was a . . ." Wade threw his hand up as the clatter of hooves burst up the trail. Patricia froze as half a dozen riders swept directly below her and up the slope.

When she was sure the riders were gone, Patricia let her breath out and Wade reached for the next branch. They proceeded from one huge tree to another for several yards until they came to a section where the large trees gave way to much smaller growths. Patricia asked, "Should we drop and continue on foot?"

"Watch me," said Wade. He climbed into the top of a tall, flexible tamarack. He swayed back and forth until he was traveling about six feet to the swing, which brought him within range of the limb of an adjoining tree. He grabbed the limb and drew the two treetops together until he could transfer to the other tree. The maneuver took some courage and a great deal of balance.

"That looks like fun," Patricia said gaily as she began the swaying motion until Wade was able to reach out and grab a limb on her tree. Working together, they were able to make good progress from treetop to treetop.

They crossed this space and got into some larger timber again. Through the limbs Patricia could make out the towering walls of a sheer cliff. They made it to a large fir tree that grew in the shale below the cliff. One lone sugar pine loomed between them and the cliff face. It reared its head upward until the top almost touched an overhang of rock.

They paused to rest in the fir. "You're quite the climber," said Wade. He pointed. "If we can get into that sugar pine, we might make it to that ledge. Trouble is we can't get into the pine even from the ground; its limbs don't start for forty feet."

Patricia sized up the situation and said, "This fir limb goes right over the lowest limb of the pine. Maybe we can make it up here."

"Yeah, but the farther you go out, the more the limb bends," said Wade. "By the time you get close to the tip, you may be nowhere near the pine branch."

"I'm the lightest. I'll go first."

"That limb will bend at such an angle that you won't be able to shinny back up if you can't grab the pine. I could at least come back, hand over hand . . . that is, if it doesn't break." Wade straddled the limb and started to inch backward. He soon saw that this would not work. Even if he could reach the lower limb with his feet, it was not stiff enough to stand on. He reversed his position and continued down the limb headfirst. He scissored the limb with his knees and pulled himself along with his hands. The limb dipped until he was able to grasp the pine limb with his hands. He kicked loose from the fir limb. His weight quickly depressed the limb on the pine to an acute downward angle.

He hung on, praying that the limb wouldn't break. He started the laborious task of going up the limb hand over hand. He progressed until he was able to throw a leg over the limb and make his way to the trunk. There he crouched and looked back at Patricia.

"If you'll climb down to the ground, I'll toss you a rope and pull you up."

"Not on your life. The lower limbs are too far from the ground. I'm coming across the way you did."

She started her slide headfirst down the limb. Sticky pitch clung to her, and sharp needles poked her face. The limb dipped perilously until all she could see was the jagged shale forty feet below. Terror gripped her. Her face paled, and beads of perspiration stood out on her forehead. She was too petrified to even cry out.

Wade could see her predicament, but there was nothing he could do. Gradually Patricia calmed her feelings and got her imagination under control. It took all her will to move. She set her jaw and began to inch downward again.

The limb drooped lower and lower until she could see that she was right over the pine branch. Yet she dangled there, sapped of strength from the climb out. She knew she couldn't put forth enough effort to duplicate Wade's feat, going up the limb hand over hand. She felt like she couldn't even cling to the limb much longer.

Wade said, "Can you get under the limb?"

Patricia nodded her head, though she was dubious of her ability to do it. As she released the grip of her knees, her body swung sideways, and the limb swayed and bobbed. Her riding skirt caught on some branches and did its own riding up. She finally made the switch and gripped the limbs with her thighs.

"Can you hang on with one hand?" asked Wade.

Patricia tightened the grip with her knees and one hand. As she raised the other one on Wade's command, he deftly lassoed it.

"Put your arm through the noose and grip with that hand."

She obeyed and, at his instruction, managed to get her head and other arm through the loop so that it rested under her armpits.

"Now, let go your hold and drop."

"Let go and drop, he says!" Patricia muttered through clenched teeth. She couldn't turn her head to see him—and she had no way of knowing what would happen if she let go. Forty feet in the air, she was supposed to forget everything and drop. But her strength was nearly gone; she couldn't hang on any longer. She took a breath, closed her eyes, and dropped.

She crashed into the pine branch below, glanced off it, and swung in a great arc toward the face of the cliff. She opened her eyes at the bottom of the swing in time to see the granite wall bearing down on her at terrific speed. Wade strained against the rope. The ascending path of that arc meant she missed the cliff by inches.

Back she went again, almost to the limb she had just vacated. She swung like a pendulum as the rope bit into her body. When her swinging died down, Wade began to laboriously haul her up towards his place on the limb, where he had tied the other end of the rope. She finally got an arm and then a leg over the branch. Once safely there, she hugged it and waited for her body to get over the shakes.

Patricia lamented, "I thought it would be fun, but you can stuff your flying, Mr. Forester!" She added between breaths, "At least now I know you can only get so scared and no more."

"I've got to hand it to you, woman," Wade said, impressed. "You've got more guts than some men. You don't develop confidence up high until you've been good and scared."

"Brother, I must literally ooze confidence!" was her only reply.

Wade looked around. "When I was a kid, we used to play in these trees all day. Many's the time I waited by the hour up high to get a shot at a wild pigeon." Another grin briefly flashed across his face.

After a rest, they climbed from limb to limb up the tree trunk. "From that ledge, we'll be able to scale up to the mesa. It's called Diamond Mesa because of its triangular shape. Uh-oh." He stopped. "This I didn't count on. From this pine I used to reach the ledge with ease. Looks like a lightning bolt knocked the top off the tree. We're far short of the lip."

They continued up to the shattered stump at the top where they stopped to breathe and consider their next move. Wade studied the cliff above. About twenty feet up a sharp spur of granite jutted out. He stood on the second highest limb of the pine and braced his knees against the one above.

"I think I can get a rope over that outcropping near the top. If the rope will hold, maybe we can climb to it and, from there, make it to the top."

He uncoiled his rope to make a try. There wasn't much room to work out a good loop. His cast went up and out but fell short. He tried again, but the rope just wasn't long enough. "Can you get up beside me?" he asked. "Take hold of my hand."

Once Patricia was on the same limb, he said, "I'm going to stand on this last limb with one foot on the stump. Hold on to my calves to steady me."

Patricia straddled the branch, gripped the trunk with her legs, and wrapped her arms around Wade's lower legs. She tried to block her doubts of how little stability this would add. Wade cast again—missed—and swooped forward as the tree swayed. He put his hand on Patricia's shoulder to steady himself. His neck grew turkey-red, and sweat stood out on his upper lip as he tried to keep his balance and cast at the same time.

He squinted carefully at the target, dropped his arm down and back, and flung a small noose at the spur. The smaller noose gave him more distance, but lowered the likelihood of a true cast. Patricia felt his legs sway and knew he had lost his balance. He clutched madly at the air with one hand but felt himself slipping. Patricia clutched his legs grimly, but she couldn't hold him and felt herself being pulled off the tree. She finally had to let go to save herself.

Wade half pivoted as his foot slipped off the branch. It was then he realized that the rope had not come tumbling back down the cliff face. He grabbed it with the other hand, unable to confirm with his eyes that his last cast had been true.

XXIII. Above & Below

It was.

Now Wade was in midair and headed for the cliff. He stuck out his feet to soften the crash against the solid granite. The impact nearly made him lose his grip on the rope.

Patricia could hardly gulp air until she realized what had happened. She watched as he braced his feet and began to walk up the side of the cliff. Soon he peered down at her from the narrow outcropping.

Now the problem was to get Patricia up. "Why didn't I bring another rope!" spat Wade under his breath as he looked up at the edge of the mesa above. If he brought Patricia up first, there'd be no room for him to throw a rope over the snag on the edge of the mesa. But there would be no point in doing that until she was on the same level, able to reach it!

"Hey," said Patricia. "Are you going to throw me the rope or leave me in this tree for the vultures?"

Wade tossed Patricia a noose, and she soon had it snug under her armpits. To avoid hitting the cliff wall as Wade had, she clung to a limb end as long as she could. With his help, she walked up the wall to the tiny outcropping.

"How do we get to the top lip?" she asked breathlessly, clutching his belt to keep from falling.

"I hate to tell you," Wade said, "but your acrobatics aren't over."

"What?"

"I need space to throw the rope onto that snag up there."

Patricia looked around. The only extra surface not already occupied was a minuscule spur of granite that didn't even look like it was solidly attached to the ledge.

She didn't say a word but faced the cliff and squatted. Holding fast again to Wade's lower shins, she gingerly let her legs down until she straddled the projecting spur.

"How's this?" she asked.

"Great, only . . ."

"Now what?"

"I, uh, I need to turn around."

Patricia looked heavenward, then she let go of his left, then his right leg, quickly replacing each hand in a vice grip after each of Wade's legs had turned. She wouldn't look down—or even up to observe Wade's throw.

After several tries, he finally got a loop over the snag. Patricia was thrilled to get off the spur as Wade climbed to the mesa. Soon a loop dangled from above, and Patricia—now an expert climber—scaled to the top.

Casting all pride aside, Patricia threw herself prone and kissed the ground. "By Aunt Bella's bustier, that's the last time I climb a tree! I wasn't sure I'd ever feel the good earth under me again—except maybe from inside a pine box."

Wade clamped his lips together, but his eyes showed amusement. "Next time you plan an aerial escape," Patricia continued, "count me out! My poor heart couldn't take it."

"We made it, didn't we?" said Wade laconically.

"I'll admit, you were right," said Patricia dryly. "My day would have been better spent with the grizzly."

Diamond Mesa proved to be little else than a freakish shelf of land, about twenty acres in extent, backed up against the sheer walls of a larger granite cliff. Across the face of the cliff a ledge ran diagonally to the top. This was the only means of access to the mesa. Water dripped from the bottom tip of this ledge all summer long.

They made camp in the shadow of this cliff, opened a can of airtight beans, and enjoyed some of Milo's sourdough biscuits. The exertion and strain of the last few hours had worn them both down. Wade lay on his back and was asleep in seconds. Patricia closed her eyes and relaxed. Just before drifting to sleep, she had time for a few wandering thoughts. They dwelt mostly on Wade. They had shared some horrible experiences. Yet in all that time, he had never looked at her as though he was interested in her as a woman. He had become more kind to her, but that wasn't difficult, considering their first conversation involved him shooting her.

***

Wade's nap lasted about an hour. Patricia slept peacefully. He knew that he must be on his way, but thought better of waking her. He lingered over her features for a minute. It was a shame she hated him; he had never known a woman with such grit. Before he left, he pulled the blanket higher on her shoulders.

He had to find a hiding place higher back in the fastness of the mountains. As night began to close, he made his way up the slanting ledge to the top of the cliff. He remembered an old mine tunnel buried in the bottom of a deep canyon. If he could find it in the dark, he would explore the drift to see if it could be a good hideout for Patricia.

He went up for a mile or two until he saw the bulk of Squaw Rock looming above him. He knew a dim trail led into the canyon on the other side. He found the mine without difficulty and was soon standing on the dump.

He needed a light, so he located a rotted pine stump and kicked it to pieces. He used his knife to shave off some pitchy slivers from the heart of the stump. He kicked a good-sized piece of pitch loose and tied it to a short stick. He made a little pile of shavings and lit them. With this fire he finally got his pitch torch to blazing. He entered the tunnel mouth with his sooty torch and began to explore. The tunnel roof dripped water on him until his shirt was damp. The persistent sound of drips was monotonous and fatigued his eardrums, but soon he was no longer conscious of the noise.

He came to a lateral shaft and turned down it for a few yards. It proved to be too wet, so he returned to the main bore. Farther on, another lateral took off to the left. He peeked in but decided it was also too wet. Beyond it, another lateral went left. It sloped upward, and the roof did not exude water. He kept on and finally came to a branch in the drift.

The fork on the right was only shoulder high and had not been timbered—as though it were only an exploratory drift that did not justify widening. If this remained dry, they could stay in it at night and be safe from intrusion.

He had gone several yards down this tunnel, looking for a place to make a bed, when he heard another sound. It was a ghostly vibration, and the echo seemed to hang in the drift; it had almost no way to dissipate. He thought it might be a trick of his imagination and almost ceased to listen for it when it came again.

The acoustics were such that he could not tell from which direction the sound was coming. He proceeded cautiously back the way he had come. The sound came again, and he stopped. It could be coming from outside of the mine. Could one of his pursuers have trailed him here? If so, he was in a tight rattrap.

He proceeded and missed hearing it for a minute or so. When it came again, he was sure it was coming from behind him. In the stygian blackness, he passed the fork he had first noticed. He retraced his steps and found it in a few short strides.

The noise came again—loudly. Wade felt his back tighten. He did not accept it as fear. There wasn't anything in these mountains, man or animal, that he was afraid of. But this was such an eerie, otherworldly tone that it prickled his scalp. Now his ears strained until he could almost feel them lengthen and stand out further from his head. The sound came again—seemingly right out of the tunnel wall. Wade jumped involuntarily and smiled sheepishly at himself. He ducked low and followed the course of the low-roofed tunnel. This was a twisting, tortuous bore. The ceiling slanted lower and lower.

Finally it ended, or seemed to come to an end. A rough, five-foot plank barred further progress. It was jammed against the low ceiling and wedged tight against the damp floor. At its base was a rock surrounded by muck. It would tax a man's strength to move. Wade dipped his torch down to examine it. As he straightened, he looked into two gleaming eyes that seemed to hang midair, between the edge of the plank and the tunnel wall. The torch lit up the deep pupils, and the whites glistened like opals.

A veritable croak of a voice said, "Is that you, Bridger, you dog? Or are you one of his scurvy gunmen?"

"It's Wade Forester. Know me?"

"I've heard of you. Get me out of here."

Stupid with surprise, Wade finally moved. He jammed his torch into a crevice, found a small board, and began to dig around the rock at the base of the plank. He finally budged the stone, then used the board to lever the bottom of the imprisoning plank until it came free from the floor. Into the firelight came a quivering scarecrow of a man, tottering on unstable legs. Wade got a hand under his armpit to support him. They moved backward slowly because the drift was so low and narrow.

In minutes they were outside in the biting, fresh air. Even in the moonlight, Wade could see the horrible condition of an emaciated, cadaver-like caricature. His hair was long and matted. The features were hatchet thin. Inflamed, watery eyes receded into deep sockets under beetling, craggy brows, and a palsied tremor shook his frame.

The man sagged against Wade and began to mumble some unintelligible gibberish. Suddenly he cried out hoarsely, "Don't, don't! Leave me alone, you rats!"

He struggled in Wade's grasp, tried to kick out, and finally slumped to the earth. Wade picked him up and carried him down off the dump. He found a bed of pine needles and lay him gently on it. Whoever he was, this victim of Bridger's penchant for torture needed care—a doctor.

The space the man had occupied was worse than the rack. It was too low to allow a man to stand upright and too narrow to allow him to sit down. The damp darkness and the loneliness—to say nothing of starvation—would upset the mental equilibrium of the sanest man.

Wade considered his options. To help this man, he must take still more risks. He had no horse, and the nearest refuge was the chief's ranch house. Could he carry the man over five miles of rough trail or should he leave him and send someone back for him on horseback? What about Patricia? What about Julia? The man groaned again, and Wade made up his mind. He picked the man up and hefted his weight. It could not have been over a hundred pounds. Wade draped the inert body over his shoulders, grasped the forearm, and set off for the chief's ranch.

XXIV. Julia

Patricia sat up suddenly. Was it a sound or just the sun hitting her face that had woken her? She had slept long and deeply. Her peripheral vision caught a movement to her left. It was an Indian. He was young, but large. When Patricia turned to look at him, he stopped, his eyes big.

Patricia was instantly self-conscious, but she asked, "Are you a friend of Wade's?"

The Indian nodded, still staring at Patricia.

"I must be a sight," she said, pulling leaves from her hair.

"A beautiful sight," said Sam Blue—now he was self-conscious—finally lowering his eyes.

"Well, thank you," said Patricia, getting up and brushing herself off. "I suppose Wade is off on another quest, or did they—"

"He's fine. He got sidetracked searching for a place for you two to hole up. Now he's gone to Carson City."

"Carson? I'm beginning to think he likes danger. He finds a safe spot, then doesn't stay in it. And what am I supposed to do?"

"Come on. You'll be safe with us."

"Us?"

***

Wade made it to the ranch house without mishap. His mind was clouded with exhaustion. Running Doe awakened and tended the old man, while Wade rested for about an hour. Again he was in the saddle. As Running Doe hastily put some corn dodgers in his saddle bag, he said, "Tell Sam Blue to head to Diamond Mesa and bring back a woman I left there." He left, leading a second horse along.

In Carson City, Wade went directly to the little home where Doctor Alexander tended Julia. When he saw it, his heart jumped into his throat. It was a flame-blackened shell. Wade's head jerked up and down the street, searching with huge eyes. He leaped from his horse. But there was clearly no one to pull out of the now-cold remnants of the doctor's home. Wade sat, right in the road, with his hands to his forehead. He was too late.

A curtain stirred in the house next door. The door opened quickly, and a middle-aged woman dashed out, looking rapidly right and left. Holding her skirt, she raced into the street to Wade. "Come inside!" she said. Mrs. Alexander grabbed Wade's hand and, leaving his horses in the middle of the street, dragged Wade up and into the house.

"Wade!" said the doctor, taking Wade's ice-cold hand. "I'm glad you're here."

"What happened? Is Julia all right?"

"She's fine. Some of Calhoun's men paid us a visit the other evening," said the doctor.

"And then they tried to blame you for the fire, Wade," said Mrs. Alexander.

"But we've seen this done before," said a short, elderly gentleman. "To some of our friends in the hills."

"This is Mr. Bercier," said the doctor. "He's been kind enough to take us in.

"We just don't understand why they would burn a house in town," said Mrs. Alexander. "We've no property of value."

"It was Julia they were after," said Wade. "Can I see her?"

"Of course," said the doctor.

Julia was in an upstairs bedroom, silently rocking before the window. Wade involuntarily called to her. "Julia."

The girl did not turn her head. It was as though she were deaf. He touched her shoulder and walked around in front of her. She looked up into his face. There was no sign of recognition.

"Dear Julia," he whispered, taking her hands and examining her. She seemed to look through him toward the window, as though he didn't exist.

"She wasn't hurt," said the doctor. "We got her out before the fire enveloped the house."

Wade stepped back and tugged at his neck, then he rumpled his hair. As happy as he was to find her safe, a helpless, impotent feeling of despair swept over him. Here was the body, the substance of a being he loved more than his own life, now a cocoon from which the butterfly had flown. Julia had been such a healthy person, more than capable of taking care of herself. Now he had to find a way to protect her when he barely had any refuge himself. Could she ever come back from that insensate pit of despond or lunacy? He was trying to grasp what could not be understood.

"Isn't there anything—any hope, Doc?"

"If there is, it eludes us. Nobody really understands the human mind."

"So, you don't know that she *won't* get well?"

"Well, no, I can't say I do. I believe her trauma to be more emotional than any physical injury that I could observe. I've seen victims of a railroad accident lose consciousness—even some memories—from physical trauma. I've also seen people stumble around in a daze who were not directly involved in any force but the horror of loss."

"A sort of self-preservation from something awful?"

"That's one possibility. When Julia was brought to us months ago, she was just as she is now. But she can hear fine; she does what she's asked to do—to the point I'm concerned the wrong suggestion might be made, and she'd end up at the bottom of a cliff or a well."

"If she's cut herself off from life to protect herself, she could still come back. I mean, she's still there, her memories and all? She's not insane?"

Doctor Alexander only nodded grimly.

"When you first wrote to me about her, I wired a specialist in San Francisco. He said if she was returned to what is familiar, it might help."

"That's not beyond the realm of possibility," said the doctor.

"I thought I was familiar enough, but I've got to get her out of here. Her life is in danger."

"I understand. You'll have to keep an eye on her. As long as food is placed in front of her, she won't starve." The doctor stepped close. "But if some trigger reaches in and unlocks whatever she's buried inside, you'll have to be prepared to deal with some rather intense emotion."

Wade nodded. "I'm so sorry to have brought you such trouble, it's all I seem to do these days. If I can ever dig my way out of this, I'll help you rebuild."

"Son, your father was my best friend. He helped me to set up my practice here. Taking care of Julia was the least thing I could do. We'll be all right. You see to your sister."

"I'm going to see if the horses are still about. Can you have her ready to travel in a few minutes?"

"Of course, Wade."

As Julia rode along beside Wade, her face remained as set as an Indian warrior's. It would be nightfall before they reached the chief's ranch.

They made good time. Running Doe met Wade at the door. Even her Indian stoicism was shaken at the sight of Julia. She had practically raised these two since the death of Anita Forester, who had passed away when Wade was about four years old. She helped Julia from the saddle and led her tenderly into the house.

Running Doe came back out while Wade was tending to the horses. He said, "I'm so sorry to keep bringing trouble to you in the time of your grief."

The Indian woman, still straight and handsome of features in spite of her sixty-odd summers, placed her hands on Wade's shoulders and looked up into his face. "My son, I never had a daughter except this one. She and you are bright lights in my visions, though I have lost children and a husband. Were the two of you my natural children, I could not love you more. Do not take from me the privilege of serving the people I love. This evil that is on the land will not last, and we will all be happy again."

"Thank you," was all Wade could say. "How is the old man?"

"He sleeps. He takes nourishment. Soon, I think, his body will be strong. But the mind? Sometimes he babbles like a baby. This, I hope, will pass. He has suffered much." Running Doe studied Wade. "You are tired." She led him from the barn to the back porch. "You must sleep."

"Has Sam returned from the Mesa?"

"They have not yet arrived. I suspect Sam Blue has taken the longer path near my people to avoid detection." She sat him on the cot behind the house. "You must rest now. They will come."

"Where is Black Wolf?"

"He scouts and prowls the hills. He is afraid we are in danger here. There is talk that the evil men have us marked for death."

"I've brought you nothing but trouble."

Running Doe covered Wade with a blanket. "When bad men make their plans, trouble comes to all. Maybe you hastened the day, but it would have come to us anyway. If it had come to us first, I know you would be here to stand with us. Now we stand together as always."

Wade slept.

XXV. Survivors

Sam Blue ushered Patricia into the living room of the chief's ranch house. There was no one there, and, as Sam had left to care for the horses, Patricia felt more than a little self-conscious.

But her mood changed as she looked around. It was a pleasing room. A few coals glowed in the fireplace, a massive pile of fieldstones that almost covered the back wall. The mantle was an enormous slab of fire-darkened fir. On the mantle was a colorful assortment of ceramics and intricate wood carvings. The walls were hung with woven blankets and pictures cleverly framed in shiny red manzanita limbs. A bowl of brightly colored gourds accented a long table.

The effect was warm and welcoming. Patricia relaxed, captivated by the obvious care and imagination that lent a dignified, yet homey feel to the place. Standing in front of the fireplace, she found herself wishing it were her home too. In all her experiences in this part of the country, she had never set foot in a real home. Now she realized that she'd never really felt at home anywhere. Her throat stiffened. This was a haven, radiating peace and security. It was a home loved by the people who lived there, people who loved each other. Patricia's eyes grew misty.

A door at her right opened, and an Indian woman stepped into the room. Her face held that patrician sereneness of one who had suffered much, but who had also loved much. She stepped over to Patricia and held out both hands. Patricia took them in hers, and they looked at each other without speaking until the silence drifted close to the edge of discomfort. The two had never been formally introduced. Finally the matriarch spoke. "I am Running Doe. And you must be Miss Laughlin. My husband told me something of you."

"This is the loveliest room I have ever seen," said Patricia, trying to smile. "It tells much about the person who furnished it—creativity, kindness, loyalty. It's the home of a true lady, in every sense of the word."

"Thank you. For one so young, you are quick to notice a loving touch—and most kind."

Patricia stepped back, self-conscious. Running Doe sensed her discomfort. "You are upset," she said softly.

"It's just that," Patricia wiped her eyes. "I'm ashamed to be taking refuge in your home after I . . . after all you've suffered."

Running Doe motioned for her to sit and fixed her eyes on hers. "We've both lost someone near to us this week."

"I know, but you . . ." Patricia wanted to change the subject. She didn't know why—it seemed such a self-centered thought coming out—but what came to her lips was, "My mother left us when I was a girl. Now there's no one." She put her head down. Running Doe put her hand on Patricia's. Patricia straightened and smiled.

There was a shuffle of feet to Patricia's left. She turned to see a bent, gray-haired man enter the room. This apparent stranger startled her. But recognition stuck her as he made his way to a convenient chair and slowly sat, gazing about with a blank look in his eyes.

Patricia went over to him, put her arms across his frail shoulders, and kissed his cheek. "Uncle Pat—where did you . . ."

The old man reached to take Patricia's arms away. Awareness seemed to dawn slowly on his face; he took Patricia's hands in his, so he could look at her. In a low voice, he said, "Is my mind completely gone or is that really you, Patricia?"

"Yes, you sweet man! It is really me." She hugged him again.

"Where am I?"

"You're safe, among friends. Can you tell me what happened to you—where you've been all these days?"

"I remember being shut up in a mine. It was Bridger Calhoun's doing. Then some man came and brought me out. That's the last thing I remember. He told me his name, but that part I don't recall. Whoever he was, I owe him a debt of gratitude."

Running Doe was standing before them, her eyes big and her mouth open. Patricia put her head down in joyful laughter, then looked at Running Doe. "He's my uncle, Pat Laughlin. How did he get here?"

Running Doe explained, as best she could, how Wade had found him and brought him in. Patricia touched her uncle's face as her expression changed to consternation. She was in deep thought. She looked up. "How in heaven's name can so-called human beings become so vile, so vicious . . ."

Running Doe took her hand and smiled. "He will be all right.

And you! Now you have someone again." Patricia's expression softened, and she sat on the floor beside her uncle.

"There's someone else you will meet tonight, someone who has not been spared any pain herself." Running Doe started out of the room. "I may as well bring her, so you can meet her yourself."

Patricia could not imagine who the woman was talking about.

Running Doe returned with Julia. She was clothed in a leather jacket and a buckskin riding skirt. Patricia stood, and Julia stared at her in what seemed to be stone-faced defiance.

As Patricia returned her gaze, she became aware that she was looking at a beautiful woman. Her features were exquisitely molded, and her complexion smooth and creamy. Her hair was a dark auburn which picked up gold glints from the lamplight. Her eyes were wide apart, large and framed by eyebrows that were perfect crescents.

Patricia stood and walked around the table to where the woman stood. She smiled a little stiffly and said, "How do you do? I don't think we've met."

The other woman gave no reply. She seemed to look right through Patricia. Patricia felt rebuffed and a little bit piqued. Her first thought was that this was Wade's girlfriend and she might feel Patricia was encroaching on her domain. Maybe the woman felt as Wade did—that Patricia was the cause of all the trouble.

Running Doe stepped to Julia's side and said, "This is Wade's sister, Julia."

Patricia thought it strange that the Indian woman did not finish the introduction by telling the woman who she was. She was also a little shocked at the silent indifference from the girl.

Running Doe said, "Miss Laughlin, Julia has completely shut down due to an experience similar to the one suffered by your uncle. For the last several months, she has not spoken a word to me, to Wade, or even acknowledged that she knew us. It's a cruel joke, worse than loss of anything, to have someone present, yet never with you."

"Oh, I . . ." Patricia's lips pressed together. "I can only apologize for my initial thoughts." Looking first at Running Doe and then at Julia, she said, "Bridger . . . Mr. Calhoun told me something of this. I just couldn't realize the impact on Miss Forester, I mean Mrs. Calhoun."

Running Doe led Julia to a chair. "Sit here, Julia," she said. Julia sat, and Running Doe stroked her hair.

Running Doe was silent for a moment and then said, "This one has been like a daughter to me. We planned and decorated this room together. She was a bright and sensitive person. She was so deeply affected by beauty, colors, and the music of nature.

"Wherever she went she brought sparkle and laughter. You think she is beautiful in repose. If you could you see that face with the fire of delight and love, then you would see true beauty."

As Running Doe turned, Patricia saw that her eyes were moist. Patricia said nothing. She was overwhelmed herself at the human drama before her—the loss experienced by each person in the room. And yet, she was sustained by the hope in the Indian woman's voice.

"Wade served her as though she were a goddess. They were closer than any two people I've ever known. Raven Eye was in love with her. Once, insanely frustrated, he insulted her at a dance, accused her of refusing to marry him because he was an Indian. Wade literally threw him out of the house. He was so angry. Before that they were like brothers. Raven Eye stayed away after that."

Patricia froze at the mention of Raven Eye. She realized that her guilt would never permit her to remain comfortable in this home, no matter how generous the inhabitants.

Running Doe watched her. "Sometimes difficult children

are sent to us from the Great Spirit to make us humble." The woman bowed her head for a minute, and, when she raised it, Patricia noted fine lines of suffering running from the ends of her nostrils around the edge of her mouth. "But life is good in a thousand ways." Running Doe smiled. "There is still so much to enjoy, so many memories, so many plans for the grandchildren I hope for."

Running Doe sat and held Julia's hand. Patricia sat with her uncle—and a stone in her stomach.

XXVI. Stunned

Wade and Sam Blue came in from the back entrance. Wade looked a little less weary as he nodded slightly and, for the first time, spoke her name, "Patricia."

"Thank you," she said, standing. Wade looked confused. "For saving my uncle." She motioned to the old man. "This is my uncle, Pat Laughlin."

Wade took his hat off and stared. He wondered if this might erase all the pain he'd heaped on Patricia, if she might somehow forgive him. All he said was, "Well, I'll be—" He was interrupted as Black Wolf entered the front door.

"How are things out there?" asked Sam Blue.

"They're closing in from below," said Black Wolf. "They're not moving fast, but they're spread out to cut us off from the side."

"The fat's in the fire for sure," said Wade. "They'll strike about morning, I'd say. Bridger pretty well knows we're all here. We've got to move out."

"But where, Wade?" asked Running Doe. "Where can we go?"

"We'll go up to the Jason Mine. If we stay here, they'll burn us out."

"I brought what I could up there," said Black Wolf. "I thought you were crazy, but now it's starting to add up."

"I'll stay here," said Running Doe. "This is my home. They won't bother me once they find you gone."

"Don't fool yourself," said Wade. "Bridger has to wipe out every person here. You know too much. Even Julia, if she ever recovered, would be a bar to his plans too. He can't leave any of us alive. We'll head for the mine. You and your boys can keep on from there until you're out of the country. Perhaps, sometime when things have quieted down, you can return. While you're out of the territory, their plans aren't threatened enough to follow you. I'm another story altogether."

Black Wolf looked at his mother with grave worry etched on his face. He looked around at the others and then spoke to Running Doe. "I'll send you over the big divide with Sam Blue. You can go to your people from there. As for me, I stay. If I live, I'll come to you there."

Sam Blue said, "Since when does my mother need a guide and a protector in the hills that our ancestors have roamed for centuries? She can go with us a ways, then slip over the divide and find the lodge of her brothers. I am not a child to be ordered about. The blood of my father cries for vengeance. I stay!"

Running Doe looked at her two sons. "It is as I suspected. We are all in this together," she said, clutching her two sons' arms. "I am too old to run, to creep back to my people for protection—people that I have not seen for twenty years. My sons are my life. If they die, I die too." As they stood, this desperate group, they were each busy with their own thoughts. Each, in his and her way, came to grips with the reality that hours might mark the span of their remaining life. There were grimaces of determination, but there was no quailing of the spirit or signs of panic.

Wade said, "Running Doe, I have to ask you to follow my instructions without question. Will you do it?"

She looked at him intently. "You are my son. I have mothered you in the absence of your own mother. I have never had cause to doubt your judgment. Why should I begin now?"

"Listen," said Wade. "Your father fought the Apache and the white man. You have heard tales of torture and the cruelty of the more savage tribes. You have seen this broken man," he motioned to Patricia's uncle. "Remember it! If the men go down, and there are none left, do what you can to protect the others." He looked at Julia, then at Patricia. "Bridger and his men have grown into savages. It may be better to die protecting yourselves than to suffer their fury."

Running Doe was resolute. "Rest easy, Wade. I have dug out the arrow and the rifle bullet from quivering flesh. I have killed with bowie knife and war ax. I am not weak as some women are weak."

"I know it," he said. "The horses are ready. Black Wolf, you scout out ahead. The old man may be too weak to ride solo, so I'll follow with him on my horse, then you three women. Sam, you'll have to watch our flank alone."

A low voice from behind them spoke out, "He won't be alone." Patricia Laughlin turned and gasped. Raven Eye leaned wearily in the bedroom doorway.

XXVII. Smoldering Sky

"You're . . ." Patricia turned to Wade with complete bewilderment on her face.

"I'm alive," said Raven Eye. Raven Eye's open shirt revealed a bandage with a little blood still seeping, but he lived and breathed before them. "You're not a murderer," he said to Patricia.

"You old fox!" said Wade, unsure whether to embrace Raven Eye or fear that he would rush out and call in Bridger's men.

"I ride to protect my family," said Raven Eye.

Wade faced him and put his hands on his shoulders. "Family," he said.

Patricia could not restrain her inquiry. "But I—"

"Running Doe pulled him through," said Black Wolf. "He's been mending here all along."

"Are you strong enough to bring up the rear with Sam Blue?" Wade asked Raven Eye.

"Saddle me a horse," said Raven Eye. "You should know by

now that I'm a taproot, not easily chopped!"

Wade and Black Wolf saddled the horses while Patricia washed and put on some borrowed clothes. The group mounted up in ghostly silence in the shadow of the house. They left a lamp burning inside, so that it would appear occupied. Wade moved out ahead, up the trail toward the mine. The stillness was only broken by the creak of saddle leather and the steady clop, clop of the horses' hooves.

They crossed the meadow, filtered through the timber and emerged onto a sage-covered slope. The trail looped across this slope making the little cavalcade a dark, twisted line against the hill. A mile or more from the house Wade breathed, "Black Wolf!" and threw up his hand so the others would stop. They strained their ears for hostile sounds. The quiet of the night was unbroken.

They dipped into a murky canyon and toiled up the other side. They were at a great disadvantage: they had to keep moving, while their enemies could simply wait for them to come into range. There was a chance there had not been time to marshal a complete force of men, but there were probably enough on hand to do the job. After a while, they paused again. Still there was no sound, only the menacing silence of the forest and the shadowy brush.

It happened as suddenly as they expected it would, in the bottom of a canyon where the moon did not penetrate. Long orange blasts of fire speared at them from both sides. The brush on each side of the trail allowed sparse cover and little room for maneuvering or flight. It was a question of continuing into the gunfire or turning tail and running to the cutoff party below.

Patricia heard her horse grunt as a ball tore into its flesh. She jumped clear as it fell into a patch of sagebrush.

Wade slid Uncle Pat from his saddle and then swept Julia to the ground. Everyone flattened out and hugged the dirt. The horses milled and stamped. Some ran up the trail and some down. Bullets crackled through the brush as they tried to ferret out their targets. The darkness was both help and hindrance to the attackers and the attacked.

No one fired a return shot. The flash would have only made a good target. Wade passed the word to crawl forward, under cover as much as possible. The trembling group tried to be silent. The firing stopped. The attackers could no longer see their targets.

"Anyone hit?" cried Wade in what should have been a whisper.

"Yeah, me!" grunted Sam Blue.

Wade attempted to crawl back to check on Sam, but Black Wolf called to him, "The old man's not moving."

Patricia heard it too. She followed Wade on all fours, tracing the trail toward her uncle. Three horses lay dead in their path. The rest had fled. When Wade lifted Uncle Pat, he felt a smear of warm blood. He leaned over and felt nothing from the mouth, heard nothing from the chest. "He's gone," he whispered to Patricia. All feeling drained from her limbs as the tears came. Another loss.

Running Doe had come after, and Wade told her to get Patricia and the others moving again as he rolled the body off of the trail.

"Julia," said Running Doe, as if calling her in from playing outside, "crawl behind me on your knees."

Black Wolf met Wade as Raven Eye came up from behind the group. "Where'd Sam Blue get to?" spat Wade. "I thought he was hit."

"He won't be comfortable sitting down for a while," said Raven Eye. "Bullet must have glanced off the cantle. He is one mad Indian!" He nodded up the hill as Black Wolf allowed himself a suppressed chuckle.

A long, piercing scream floated on the air and ended in a gurgling sob. Wade turned toward the scream. "I thought knives were supposed to be quiet," he said. "At least Bridger's men won't stay so close now."

They all moved ahead on hands and knees for another hundred yards. They heard a rustle of brush, and Sam Blue was with them again.

Wade said, "If we separate a little, we won't be such good targets. We'd better split up for mutual protection. I'll lead off with Julia. Black Wolf, stay with Patricia. Sam Blue, no more lone-wolfing; you're to stay with your mother. Wait! Listen."

They heard the unmistakable sounds of horses moving away from the ambush sight. A voice floated up to them. "We've got them afoot; they can't go much higher without bumping into Gila Red's bunch. Curly, ride down to camp and get Bridger. He shoulda been up here by now. Tell him come daylight, we'll have 'em all for sure."

Another voice said, "It don't pay to crowd 'em too much in the dark. Them injuns can get you against the sky and ventilate you good. Somebody in that crowd is mighty handy with a knife. Watch your back trail."

Wade and his party hiked cautiously up toward the mine for another mile without mishap when Wade called another halt. "Sam Blue, Raven Eye, hang back with the others while Black Wolf and I scout ahead a bit."

They disappeared for what seemed to Patricia to be hours. When they returned, Wade said, "They're waiting for us up ahead. They heard the firing and have a nice surprise set up, in case we got through. We'll go down Little Beaver Canyon and up the other ridge."

There was no trail now to follow. They had to find their way through rugged and steep country. They closed into a tight group with Black Wolf in the lead. He best knew the terrain and how to find his way through the opposing brush. They reached the crest of the ridge and found the going easier.

It was grueling work and required rest intervals for tired

muscles and burning lungs. The occasional patches of timber were a respite from the spiny brush. Under the trees they moved with less effort and were able to proceed more rapidly. They came out into a sizable opening, and all sat or squatted for a well-earned rest. Suddenly, Patricia stood. "Look!"

Far below them, the darkness was split by the unmistakable flare of a large fire. Running Doe stood too. "Home," she said quietly.

Patricia's face showed utter heartbreak. Her voice vibrated with rage. "Those degenerate pigs!" The warmth and comfort of that one room made an indelible picture in her mind's eye. Now, a gaunt, blackened chimney would be a monument to stupid, unbridled avarice.

XXVIII. Demons

They moved on. Finally, through the trees, they could see the blue whiteness of the mine dump shining in the moonlight.

On the dump, close to the adit, were the mine buildings. The bunk house was to the left of the tunnel and the powder shed beyond against the hill. The cook shanty was to the right of the mine opening. In front of the adit was the toolshed and blacksmith shop.

Wade ushered the women into the bunkhouse. "Get some rest while you can," he told them. "There's little chance of an attack before dawn." He knew Bridger would take his time, now that he knew his prey was cornered.

Wade said, "I need someone to give me a hand outside. Feel like a little work, Black Wolf?"

"Why not?" said Black Wolf. "Exercise is good for your health . . . and I've been worried about mine, not sure it'll last the rest of my life."

Julia, impervious to the tension in the air, had immediately gone to sleep on a bunk. Raven Eye came in, saw that she was asleep, and exited without a word.

Patricia tried to force herself to relax, but her nerves wouldn't let her. Running Doe was putting a bandage on Sam Blue's lacerated hip.

Sam Blue said, "Don't bother with anything fancy. It probably won't have to last me very long anyway, after these butchers get through." His mother gave him a look, but he only laughed. "Who wants to live to be a stove-up old man anyway? May as well go out in smoke as rot in some hospital bed. A slow death never did appeal to me."

Wade came in triumphant. "I found some beans in the cook shack and fired up the stove, if anyone wants some. They'll do you good."

"I could eat," said Patricia, rising. "I'm certainly not sleeping."

Wade turned to Sam Blue. "Looks like you'll have to eat off of a high shelf."

"Yeah. I always thought I'd get it in the end," said Sam Blue. "I heard'a people with lead in the pants; seems I got mine the hard way."

Black Wolf came in and said, "If you're planning on eating, better make it fast. The birds are talking it up. It'll be light soon. I figure they'll make their play once it's nice and bright."

They woke Julia and brought her to the cook shack. In a half hour, the food had helped most of them to relax a little. Black Wolf brought in some bundles, and Wade said, "Now look, everyone, Black Wolf stashed some rifles up here just in case, so we're not unarmed. Don't make any kind of a play until I give the signal. There'll be plenty to shoot at. Let's not get anxious or trigger-happy. Bridger will probably want to palaver and gloat. He might go for some kind of a deal; wiping us out wouldn't leave him in the best of positions. He knows that such things get around. You can't keep a secret that a hundred men know. His only hope is to gain so much power he can smother any investigation."

Black Wolf said, "I can knock him out of the saddle at four hundred yards. You decoy him in, and I'll perforate his gizzard. Get him and there won't be much use for the gang to finish the job, 'that I guarantee!'"

"No," said Wade. "I need to talk to Bridger before anything happens. Is that understood?"

The brothers nodded their heads. Sam Blue said, "It's your show, Wade. Play her the way you want. I'll tell you one thing, if I get out of this alive, there's going to be the darnedest one-man war you ever heard of. I'll prowl these hills the rest of my life. Every mother's son of that crowd that gets in my sights will be dead, and none will sleep peacefully while they wait."

"Have you learned nothing from your older brother?" spat Raven Eye. "Do you want to end up like me—bitter, vengeful? Our father is dead because of my careless, selfish—"

"Brothers!" said Black Wolf in a low exclamation. "Our family needs our protection. As long as they are with us, we must keep watch and keep free of vengeful or selfish actions."

Sam Blue sat—but quickly stood again, wincing. Wade put his foot on a chair and stared at nothing. No one spoke.

Patricia wished she could face death with a flippant jest, like Sam Blue. Fear gripped her vitals and pushed them weightily in her abdomen. There was a tremor in her fingertips and an obstruction in her throat that no amount of swallowing could dissipate.

Excepting Julia, perhaps, the others had faced death many times until it was no longer a stranger to them. They could go out to meet it with a grim smile and a devil-may-care insouciance. On top of Patricia's fear of physical harm was a fear more potent and more awful than the contemplation of death. The horrible thought that stabbed at her mind was the possibility that, when the chips were down, she could not face her doom without groveling and showing the white feather. She envied Julia's blankness of imagination.

The good opinion of these people had become of paramount importance to Patricia. It was true that, going down with her, they would likely not live to remember her cowardice, but she desperately wanted to be worthy to die with them—like them— with calm bravery. She was too wise to believe that she would will herself not to break. She knew that, in a crisis, it is the character and habits of many years that determine how one will act in a moment. And no one knows the depths of his or her emotions until the fiery test burns all around. She was afraid of what she didn't know about herself: How would she face death?

This fear of herself was worse than any outside threat. Her impulse was to run, now, and never face that hour of decision. It seemed almost easier to take a bullet in the back, while in headlong flight, than face the crisis head-on. It was an instinct—a basic drive for self-preservation. Why not flee into the brush and hide from this fate that seemed so certain?

She looked, one by one, at the serene faces about her. None of these people seemed to show any concern for the immediate future. They entered blandly into everyday talk about things extraneous to the decisions of the moment, as if tomorrow would come and life would flow as usual. She studied them.

A muscle quivered and pulled at the angle of Wade's jaw. Under Black Wolf's folded arms, his knuckles held little color, his hands were so tight. There was a falseness to Sam Blue's grin that made it almost a smirk. Because they were men, it was expected that they not show any outward sign of revulsion for that shadow that wipes away the future. Running Doe tidied the shack—a place they would not return to regardless of today's outcome. Raven Eye stared out the window, despite the mostly dark sky. Death was no picnic for them, no matter how many times they had faced it.

It was then that Patricia felt a strong kinship with these

people—a bond of unity that made their determination hers. It made her want to shout, "I'm one of you. I feel what you feel!" This, then, was to be her solace and her comfort. She had the sure knowledge that they would face this travail together, with an unspoken understanding that they would never let an enemy gloat over the sight of them groveling or begging for mercy.

A quick pride welled up in Patricia at the thought that she should be counted among these souls. An effulgent, inner radiance seemed to pervade her being. She knew that if, by some miracle, they should elude destruction, there would forever be a warm camaraderie among them that would never be forgotten.

She spoke up soberly, "Some of my creditors are sure going to be unhappy to hear I've gone away without paying up." Adding flippantly, "And with no forwarding address to boot! Tsk. Such bad business." She pressed her lips in a smile.

Wade smiled back at her. His look was different toward her now. Might he have realized that she wasn't the villain he'd accused her of being? It came to Patricia that he could have been suffering for her just a little, feeling that she might not be strong enough to face the coming ordeal. Her glib lightness told him that she would be a good soldier and not come apart when the going got really rough.

The boys threw Patricia an appreciative glance, and she knew that she was accepted as an equal. The raw certainty settled into her being that she was indeed made of that stern stuff required to face one's fate bravely. She was not afraid to be afraid.

Wade stood, handed out the rifles, and gave instructions. He and the brothers went to their assigned posts outside. Running Doe and Patricia were to see that no one got through to Julia.

Their wait wasn't long.

XXIX. A Sky So Big

A body of horsemen charged at the sharp rise below the dump at a dead run. They did not slow for finesse or deployment. They were too sure of their quarry for that. The earth shook as they came pounding to the level flat on top of the tailings pile. They pulled up as one body in front of the blacksmith shop. The horses squatted behind stiffened forelegs as their masters sawed on the cruel bits. Bridger's magnificent black stallion jerked its head and pawed the ground. Bridger, quite relaxed, rode masterfully in the saddle. He shouted in a triumphant, authoritative voice, "Come out, Forester. Let's powwow."

Wade stepped out through the side door of the shop. He apparently had no weapon except the Colt, which was not much of a threat against this multitude. There were about twenty men in the posse before him, and another twenty or more behind them down the trail. Wade could see other horsemen up the hill behind him at his left, waiting for a signal to close in. He rested one foot on an empty carbide drum and said, "I'll listen. It's your party."

Several guns came out, but Bridger waved a hand. "No shooting, boys, until I give the word. There's only three able-bodied men there, but they've still got a little bite. No sense in some of us getting killed if they're crazy enough to put up a fight." He grimaced at Wade with malevolence.

Back in the cook shack, Patricia had to remind herself to breathe. The opposition was comprised of tough, hard-riding men whose consciences had long been seared silent. Wade's figure seemed so pitifully small and alone, at the mercy of superior numbers. But Patricia saw no hint of retreat in his silhouette.

"You must have the brains of a porcupine," said Bridger to Wade. "Letting yourself get trapped this way, and to do it with people you care about—people entirely innocent of wrongdoing. I confess, you pulled one over on us last night. I had you figured for an attempt over the Sierras; you'd never have made it, but the try would have been more sensible than this. Dumb ox, you were licked from the start, you know. I'd have cooled you down in Carson that day, if you'd have had the guts to go for your gun."

"That would have been smart, wouldn't it?" said Wade. "You had a man in every doorway. Your hired killers do your work for you. You've never met a man in a fair gun battle in your life. It's more your speed to pick on helpless women."

Bridger's lips parted; he seemed at the point of giving the signal for a concerted rush, but he spat tobacco juice instead. "You talk big for a whipped dog." He leaned forward. "I'm ready to make a deal with you."

"Any deal you ever made was so crooked, it would break a snake's back to follow it."

"I'll give you a choice. You can surrender, or we'll roast you in that shack in the hottest fire this side of hell. If you retreat to the mine, we'll blast the exit and let you suffocate."

"What happens if we surrender?"

Bridger leaned forward in anticipation, like a hungry panther. "First, I want that dark-haired wench that clouted me with a poker. She won't be so high and mighty once she's been made to eat a few of those choice expressions she used on me." He straightened. "Then I have some papers for her to sign."

Bridger looked at the sky. "For you, I should hang you for all the people you've murdered." He looked back at Wade. "But I think I'll find a nice nest of warrior ants and spread you over it—perhaps with a garnish of molasses to whet their appetites."

Wade said acridly, "If you're through blowing off like a potbellied whale, I'd like some questions answered. I wanna start that long sleep with a few mysteries cleared up, if you'll indulge me."

Bridger took his hat off and put it to his chest. He was enjoying his hour of triumph. "Anything for a bosom friend. Shoot."

"Not that it makes any difference now, but I'd like to know for the record who ordered the job on my horse the first time my camp was raided."

Buzz Diaz snickered with his chin to his chest. "Why I heard about that," said Bridger. "Pity, but the way you burn through horses, you don't mean you want me to believe this one meant something to you?"

Wade ignored the reply. "Who took a shot at Patricia in Gardnerville?"

"Why, Gila Red." Bridger looked around him. "Never was that good of a shot, Gila. I s'pose that's why he's nowhere in sight."

"What about the chief?"

"Curly Hansen handled that. Raven Eye wasn't in on it, though he may as well have been. It was his scouting that turned up the information. But I understand he's past feeling guilt—or anything else for that matter." Bridger chuckled.

Raven Eye had kept out of sight, but he almost tore out of

his hiding place, rifle blazing, when he heard Bridger insinuate that he knowingly provided information that led to his own father's death. Bridger was wiping his own bloody hands on him, and it made him fume.

"And my father?" asked Wade.

"He was coming down from this mine with a mule train of high-grade. We jumped him, and he made a run for it. He holed up behind a bluff—did real well until his ammunition ran out. When we closed in, he got real stubborn and nasty. He called me a yellow-bellied suck-egg. I guess he made me kinda mad. He didn't even beg—just kept cussing me out till I shot the words out of his mouth."

"Dad always knew how to call it like it is," said Wade, looking down. "How about Julia?" He didn't look up.

"Mule-headed like the rest of the tribe," spat Bridger. "I took her through the whole marriage to-do in San Francisco. After a few months, I tried to persuade her to put the ranch in my name. Well, I guess she didn't love me enough. After a slap fight, I finally told her she was living in sin—that we weren't really married. The next day she lost the baby . . . and her marbles. I didn't have to twist her arm after that to sign the deed transfer. Oh, she signed them—nice and legal, witnesses and all. Of course, she was a little out of sorts by that time."

Wade's features warped until his bared teeth glistened like the fangs of a snarling, trapped wolf, but he didn't move.

Bridger laughed, the booming sound echoing against the hills. "That last part finally got you riled, didn't it?"

For an intense moment, it seemed as though Wade were contemplating charging the whole bunch on his own. But he finally put both hands on his belt buckle and spoke again in an even tone. "And what happened to Patricia's father? Raven Eye and Whitey Cross said he'd been killed more than a month ago, but that doesn't stack up."

Bridger chuckled. "I think I'll let you ask him in hell when you see him. It won't hurt you to die with one mystery stuck in your craw, though it was pure inspiration, if I do say so myself. You'll piece it together. It's a dog-eat-dog world, Wade. I learned that when they killed my pa over a stupid silver claim. If a man doesn't take what he wants, by fair means or foul, he'll end up having what he has taken away. Well, you know how that feels."

XXX. To Swallow the Earth

In the cook shack Patricia took in this horrendous spectacle of a man. Here was arrogance and brutality beyond her capacity to comprehend.

Running Doe shoved shells into the loading gate of a Winchester. When she finished she looked over and thrust the rifle into Patricia's hands. Patricia looked down at it. Its weight, far from uncomfortable, represented her chance for life. She looked at Running Doe and was a little shocked to see the usual gentle serenity replaced by an almost fierce grimness of determination. Patricia heard Wade say, "Make your play Bridger. You'll have to do it the hard way."

Bridger's horse was restive from the spur. It danced and fretted as Bridger wheeled and turned in front of his men. He stopped his horse with a cruel jerk on the Spanish bit. But he had reined it to one side of his warrior group, as if to give them room where he dared not go.

His eyes darted between them and Wade while he spoke. "That digger squaw is here with her whelps, I suppose. Too bad about their pa and that fine house, but they signed the deed and everything over when they followed you." He turned to his men. "I've told Slim not to play with matches; he just doesn't listen!" The men laughed, and Bridger looked back at Wade, raising his voice. "I'll give you all one more chance to surrender the whole shebang. Then I'm coming in behind plenty of lead. You know you haven't got a chance, that I guarantee."

Wade's self-restraint snapped. He shouted hoarsely, "Come and get us, you carrion eater!"

One of Bridger's gang got trigger-happy and thumbed off a shot. Patricia saw Wade double over like a jackknife and he fell forward. She had time for the one hopeless thought that he was killed and this was the end, when the roof seemed to blow off of the earth. The concussion of a terrific explosion smashed out a pane of glass at her side. Julia started for the first time. Patricia reeled back and heard the thunder of clods, rocks, and rubble raining to the ground and the tin roof. She ran to the door, rifle still in hand, and burst out into the open.

Where the front body of riders had been was a huge cloud of dust that obscured her vision. Patricia saw a horse still rolling end over end down the steep slope of the dump, in pursuit of the scattering horses that had remained farther back, their riders powerless to contain them. As the dust cloud dissipated, she saw a writhing mass of horses and men floundering around on the dump. The hair on her neck prickled as a horse screamed in agony. Curly Hansen lay dead, his body ripped up by the blast. Some survivors were swearing, screaming, and struggling under downed horses. There was the rank smell of powder smoke mingled with fresh blood. From then on, the action was so confused and rapid she only had a vague memory of what transpired.

Wade straightened from his stooped position behind

the carbide barrel. He snatched a rifle from the ground and wheeled, yelling toward the smithy, "If Bridger's still alive, leave him to me!"

As Black Wolf and Sam Blue closed in from the side of the blacksmith shop, Patricia found herself following after. Running Doe fired out the window at the men up on the slope, who quickly scrambled over the rise for cover. Raven Eye picked some off from his vantage point a ways up behind the shack.

Shots began to cross the tangle of men and horses at the explosion site—from within, from behind cover of the ridge, and from Wade and the chief's family. Patricia's mind shouted for her to reverse course even as her legs propelled her forward. She was open to searching lead from many directions. The thought was dispelled by a seething defiance of her would-be killers. She thought of her father, her Uncle Pat, and those at whose side she now fought. Bridger's men still had the choice to hightail it out of there if they had any qualms about fighting for a lowlife like Calhoun. Some did.

The rifle bucked in her hands; she worked the lever with frantic speed. The barrel grew hot to her touch. Then the hammer fell on an empty chamber. The rest was nightmare. Hands grabbed at her, and she clubbed at them and the heads of their owners with the rifle butt. It was a melee of dust, blood, screams, and curses.

Gila Red scrambled behind the cook shack, kicking in the back panels while Running Doe was reloading. Julia didn't scream, and Running Doe wouldn't. She lifted her rifle to club Red, but he threw her to the floor, extracting a knife from his belt. After killing the Squaw, he was going to make Bridger a bona fide widower. But his knife never reached Running Doe or Julia. Raven Eye dove at Red's hips from outside the shack. They tussled, and Red's knife found place in Raven Eye's lower back. It wasn't enough to keep the Indian, knife still in him, from crushing Red's windpipe with a rifle.

Finally, three survivors of the blast stood with their hands in the air, then quickly sat on the ground trying to stanch the flow of blood from an assortment of wounds. Bridger was found over at the side, pinned under his horse and motionless. Sam Blue was the nearest one to him. He wiped blood from a long skinning knife and walked over to where Bridger lay, horse legs draped over him. He prodded the body with a rough toe but got no response.

Black Wolf approached Wade. "Watch out for those circle riders. They're probably regrouping down the hill."

"What?" shouted Wade.

Black Wolf lifted his voice, "The group down the hill, they may be back!"

Wade walked over to one of the men who had escaped serious injury. He practically shouted, "Ride down there and tell them that Calhoun is dead and, if they close in, there's no one to pay any wages for finishing this thing." The man staggered toward a lone, only slightly injured horse and rode down to tell the riders it was over.

"You can't hear, can you?" said Black Wolf.

"All right," said Wade. "I'll catch my breath in a minute." Black Wolf chuckled.

"There's no one to pay you if you're still up there," Wade shouted up the ridge, unsure if anyone remained on the other side. "We won't pursue you if you crawl out of here now!"

Wade wiggled a finger in his ear, then strode over to Bridger and watched him closely. The man was still breathing. Patricia approached, peering at Bridger. Wade turned to Patricia soberly and said loudly, "Would you bring Julia?"

As she entered the shack, Patricia froze. Though Julia was unaffected by the two dead men on the floor, Running Doe was stroking Julia's hair, as if trying to comfort her.

After leading Julia to Wade, Running Doe grabbed Bridger by the hair and slapped him sharply across the face. Finally a deep, resonant sigh escaped from his lips. Bridger's eyes slowly opened until he was gazing sightlessly into the sky.

As Bridger's consciousness returned, he became aware of Wade standing grimly before him. Next to Wade was Sam Blue with the long knife bare, blood-smeared, and menacing in his hands. Beside Sam Blue was Running Doe, still fierce in her expression. "Raven Eye is dead," she said. And then her tears came.

Bridger couldn't make sense of that phrase. Wade's head went down. Then he looked at Julia. He took her hand and led her toward Bridger, then sat her face-to-face with her onetime husband. She shrank back at the sight of the dead horse. This was the first feeling Wade had seen in her since his return. Wade kept firm hands on her shoulders as Julia shook her head violently until her hair hung in a tangled mat over her face. "It's Bridger, Julia. Bridger! Look at him."

Wade stepped back with a hopeless, helpless look on his face. Running Doe's face softened in an expression of maternal empathy. Patricia, still shaken by the ordeal of the battle, witnessed this scene with a feeling of impotence. Her mind strained with intense hope, wanting with her might for rationality to return, for awareness to register on Julia's face. She prayed.

Julia's expression was unchanged, but her gaze was settled on Bridger's contorted face. Now it was Bridger who sought escape. He seemed to shrink back, hugging the body of the dead horse. His voice was airy with terror as he whined, "Give me a chance. I'm all broken up." He raised his only free hand. "Get this horse off of me, Wade, and I'll sign everything over to you. Don't k—" The words caught in his throat. "Don't kill me in cold blood. I'll make everything right again. I'm paralyzed." The timbre of his voice rose as he begged, "Help me. Julia, help me!"

Julia's head began to move on her shoulders. Her fists

clenched and unclenched, and she began to sway from side to side. Bridger's groveling pleading was directed straight at her.

"Julia, Julia, don't let them kill me. I love you, and you love me. We can be together again. Please, please. They're going to murder me. Don't let them!"

Julia's head stopped its motion. She frowned, frozen as though in deep concentration. A low dawning, that only Bridger saw, appeared in her eyes. A barely audible whisper escaped her lips. "Bridger. Bridger Calhoun." She leaned closer and fixed her eyes on Bridger, expressionless.

"You cannot swallow the earth," she finally murmured, turning her head. "Wo unto them that join house to house! That lay field to field till there be no place that they may be placed alone in the midst of the earth . . ." Her voice faded.

Suddenly every eardrum was blasted and every nerve jumped as a scream that tore from Julia's throat. It was sheer horror with the explosive force of long pent-up emotion. It came again, dying off in a hoarse, dry sob.

In a flash of blurred action, she rolled backward, kicking at Bridger's face as she scrambled away from him. Her visage contorted in terror. She remembered fear, and she continued to kick the dirt as if to fend off a venomous snake about to strike her.

She began screaming, "Cowardly, dirty, filthy brut!" Tears streamed down her cheeks as Wade knelt putting his arms around her protectively. Julia shook and trembled from the agitation within her.

Wade pulled her to him and away from the object of her horror. She seemed to stiffen again. A look of tenderness and longing took the place of the terror. She threw herself toward Bridger and began sobbing, "Bridger, Bridger?" She straightened abruptly. "No!"

Wade reached down and pulled her up again. She looked around like a cornered lynx, tore herself out of Wade's grasp, and fled like a deer down the steep slope of the mine dump. Near the bottom, she fell full length and slid to a stop in the loose gravel. She recovered her feet and ran into the brush-filled canyon.

Wade and Black Wolf followed after her, trying to contain her destructive dervish. She smashed into the brush, leaving small strips of clothing clinging to the thorns as they scratched her skin. She would stumble and crawl, then heave to her feet as the men came close, only to go down again. She flailed at the brush with her arms, heedless of the sharp spines as she fought.

Now she ran out of the canyon. At the foot of the dump, she came to a halt. She stiffened, then she and crumpled to the ground, rolling down the slope, then stopping, as still as death.

As Wade knelt beside Julia, a movement flicked in the corner of Patricia's eye. She swung her head sharply, causing the others to follow her gaze. For seconds they stood immobilized at a sight that was almost unbelievable. It was the sort of tale that would subsequently be told by old-timers around hearth and campfire for many years to come—first to Wade, who would miss it entirely.

Bridger had freed his left arm and moved his torso until his right leg wriggled out. The inert weight of the horse was still sprawled across his left leg. On his back, Bridger pressed his free foot against the horse's chest. His great muscles knotted and strained. The veins stood out on his forehead like cords until he freed his pinned leg. In one movement he rolled onto his belly, scooped a rifle from the ground, and leveled it at Patricia.

The stunned group stared. To Patricia, this lethal bore looked as large as the end of a stovepipe. Though he was breathless, the feral warping of Bridger's face left no doubt as to his murderous intent. But the gun had hardly reached his shoulder when Running Doe, like an arrow from the bow, sprang in three racing, silent bounds, directly into the mouth of the menace.

Bridger let the hammer fall as Running Doe knocked the

barrel away. Her skinning knife came up in a swift arc, but Bridger fended off the thrust, then swung the butt of the gun around and struck Running Doe's shoulder with a glancing blow that sent her sprawling into Bridger's dead horse.

Sam Blue's reflexes were only slightly slower than his mother's. No sooner had Bridger struck Running Doe then he was smashed by Sam Blue, whose momentum rolled them both along the ground.

Sam's rapier-like blade found its mark by chance. He pulled back and grabbed at the rifle barrel with his left hand, only to discover the blade in Bridger's neck.

"Must have lodged in his vertebrae," he said as he finally snapped it off at the hilt. "From the Great Chief and my brother. Let my knife stay buried with you." But Bridger was beyond hearing or caring.

Patricia's impulse was to turn away, but she only stared at the broken corpse.

XXXI. Masks

Patricia's trance was broken as Running Doe scrambled up from the ground and came toward her. Patricia had instinctively liked this matriarch from their first acquaintance. Now she knew this woman could charge into the very muzzle of death to protect the ones she loved. Perhaps this mother had reacted without thinking and would see nothing strange or wondrous about her courageous act.

Running Doe ripped a sleeve from her own exquisite shirt and began wrapping Patricia's bleeding hand. Patricia hadn't noticed the wound and had even less of an idea of how she got it. In Patricia's heart, there would forever be a deep affection for Running Doe.

Down the slope Wade was seated next to Julia, his arms protectively around her. Black Wolf helped them to their feet and guided them into the bunkhouse where they laid Julia on a bed. Her skin was gouged, scratched, and bruised. Her tangled hair was peppered with sticks, leaves, and red dust. Her eyes closed. Her face was a pasty, bluish gray, and her breath came slowly, so shallow it was hardly discernible.

Wade pulled up a stool and sat facing Julia. Patricia, weak and shaky from days of scrambling and fighting, sat on the edge of another bunk to support Wade in his vigil. His face grew long with sadness. He did not take his eyes off of that pallid countenance but gazed on it with intense concentration, as though he were trying, with all the strength of his will and mind, to bring those eyes open with the spark of sanity he so hoped for.

He took Julia's hand and stroked it softly. As Wade concentrated, there came a tremor and a slight flutter to Julia's eyelids. He pushed back the matted hair from her forehead. Her eyes remained closed, but there was pronounced movement under those lids. He leaned forward and turned his ear. Faintly, softly, he heard an ethereal syllable, "Wade."

"I'm here, Julia," he coughed. "I'm right beside you. You're safe."

Her eyelids twitched and cracked open. Her voice was stronger now, and there was an urgent hope in the tone. "Oh, it's . . . I was so afraid it wouldn't be you." She sobbed and pulled his hand to her face.

She moved as though to rise, her eyes wide now as love lit her face anew. Wade slipped an arm behind her shoulders. Slowly her arms crept up his arm and clamped hard behind his neck. "You're real. You're solid flesh. It's not a dream."

Wade held her tenderly with his cheek against her hair, rocking her and stroking her back. "Oh, Wade, I've missed you like you'll never know. Please don't ever leave again."

A sudden weakness seized him. He seemed to be coming apart in the middle. He could not speak. The tightness in his throat finally released a deep sob that shook them both. Julia looked at her brother, stroked his scabbed and stubbled cheek, and said with some concern, "It's all right now, Wade. We're together. Don't be sad."

To Wade it seemed so unreal—after so many days and nights of running, dodging for cover, fighting at every turn, and losing people dear to him—then to have such a terrible wrestle to reclaim his sister from an abysmal pit. This single torture had pecked at his mind, taunted his every faculty. But he had never stopped trying. Now he held the reward for all of his worry and care.

Patricia covered her mouth, reluctant to show the mix of empathy and elation at the miracle she was witnessing. She understood now the terrible strain that had gnawed on Wade.

Wade gently lowered Julia to the pillow and said, "Rest now. You've had a big day, but everything is going to be all right. Leave everything to me."

She clung to his hand, a little anxiety returning to her face. "This is real, right? I'm not imagining this."

"All is well. I'm here, and I'm not going anywhere. Just sleep." Wade stood but kept his eyes on Julia. Running Doe came in and sat on the bed. Julia smiled and closed her eyes as her adopted mother kissed her face. She sank back on the pillow and made her way into a peaceful, normal sleep.

Patricia, now self-conscious of her presence, rose from the bunk and made her way outside. She walked up the hill near the mine exit and sat on a convenient rock. She looked out over the blue haze of the valley in the distance and thought of the tumultuous events that had transpired since she came to this country. Her mind went from spinning to sadness, then finally, peace.

In a few minutes her reverie was broken by Wade, who came up to where she sat. He squatted on the ground and dug at the soil with a twig.

"How's Julia?"

"What? Oh, she's asleep," he said.

"I understand many things now that I didn't see before."

"Hindsight isn't a gift," he said.

"I see now why you didn't fight Bridger in Carson."

"He was technically my brother-in-law, or so I was led to believe. I knew he had something to do with Julia's condition, and I thought he might have a part in getting her back to normal. He had big plans. If they had materialized, my ranch would have become a lake and all the land in the valley below would have been rich, irrigated farmland."

"I guess I hold title to most of that worthless desert."

"It may not be as worthless as you think. Bridger's plan was sound. It was just that he wanted it all for himself, regardless of who he hurt to get it. He would have cheated the farmers, charged them exorbitant prices for the land and the water."

"I was so blind—so sure you had killed my father. Of course I know now that you couldn't have. I suppose Bridger was the guilty one. I just wish I knew what really happened to him."

"I think I've figured that out. There's a deep ice cave back there in the hills. I think Bridger put him in there and let him freeze to death. Then, when he wanted to frame me, all he had to do was thaw out the preserved body and make it look like a recent killing. He was fiendishly clever—almost made it work."

"When I think of how close I came to killing you, it makes me shudder inside. I never knew I could . . . When I get back to San Francisco, perhaps I can put all this horror from my mind."

Wade stood slowly. He looked down at Patricia until she looked back up at him. He said, with some hesitation, "I've been meaning to ask your forgiveness. I was pretty rough on you—just about every time we crossed paths."

"We've been through quite an adventure!" Patricia smiled and stood. "I truly respect your courage in the face of what must have seemed so overwhelming at every turn."

"You've shown a heap of grit yourself!" He smiled briefly. "I don't know how to put the words together. Somehow I feel you belong in this country. I know it's raw and only partly civilized, but, if you were around long enough, I know you would grow to love it as I do. With your help, I could make your father's dream something that benefits the whole community—what he probably had in mind from the start. I'm sure he wanted it for you."

"My father was a good, kind man. He didn't get mixed up with Bridger intentionally—at least, I'm sure he didn't know who he'd partnered with. He was too trusting, incapable of recognizing that men can sometimes become monstrously selfish. It took a shock to make me see through Bridger's smiles and polite talk. I almost fell for it all." She stared off toward nothing. "I never imagined I could face so much evil—not just in him, but in myself. I hated you from the beginning."

"Well, I wasn't exactly sending you valentines. I thought you were a scheming, calloused—"

They both turned at the sound of footsteps behind them. Running Doe stopped and stared at them with an amused expression.

"I didn't mean to eavesdrop, but I couldn't keep quiet when I caught your words about hate. Foolish children, don't you know that love is sometimes masked by hate? The reason you hated each other beyond the demands of the real circumstance was for a much deeper reason. You two are the same. Patricia, you are much woman, Wade is much man; the Great Spirit made two people with rare gifts of courage and a vast capacity for love. Why do you stand here making polite talk, pretending you are blind to your deepest feelings? Patricia's eyes make a big talk whenever she looks at you, Wade. And you, you big stupid badger, where is your head? You couldn't track an elephant in a snowstorm. If you could read, you'd know where the trail leads." She turned. "I have said enough. Now you'll be blaming me for all the petty quarrels and misunderstandings that come to all couples in love."

As Running Doe walked away, Wade looked at Patricia with a softer, more vulnerable expression than Patricia had ever seen on him. He wanted to pull her into his arms with his regular roughness. Instead, he touched her good hand. Patricia withdrew it, lifting it to caress his poor, battered face.

THE END

Genoa, named after the Italian city (though not pronounced the same), was settled by Mormons (Latter-day Saints) in 1851 when Nevada was still part of the Utah Territory. It served as an outpost on the California trail and was Nevada's first permanent, non-native settlement. Later, in the south, Las Vegas was made an outpost for Mormons traveling between Utah and Southern California.

A Barn Full o' Proud

A short story
by Ransom A. Wilcox

You might say, for the times, I was a typical ranch boy. I could ride a bare-back horse at a flat-out run when I was eight years old. It wasn't long before I could herd our cows into the corral while standing on the horse. When I was fourteen I was doing a man's work and earning a man's pay.

Feeling sorry for myself was not one of my weaknesses. But this morning I was close to it. It was my birthday. By the time my dad and mom were up, I was already dressed. I looked directly at them as they said, "Good morning, David." I was disappointed but shrugged it off. They were hard-working ranch people trying to make a go of a small acreage. Even after my accident they treated me the same (maybe they were a little more un-feeling than I thought they should be). It seemed to me that my older sister got most of the attention. At least her clothes cost more.

But I knew where to find genuine love. She was the most beautiful thing God ever made—sure as you're born. I'll tell you how I came to fall in love.

Dad used to hire out each summer to come up with extra money for taxes. A couple of summers back I joined him, working for a rancher we called "Big Bill" Baldwin.

It took plenty of hay to feed his cattle; seems like I spent months driving Dad's team with a mower 'round and 'round the alfalfa fields. The Pitman arm would chatter as it worked the blade back and forth across the stems. From the standpoint of looks, old Son and Tad weren't much to brag about, but they were stayers. The railroad had put a stage line out of business. This team had been the leaders in a six-horse hitch. Now they looked a little drawn, and you could count their ribs.

After a few days of drying, hay was raked into windrows. Sometimes a baler followed down the rows and kicked out neatly-baled hay. But some hay was stacked. A tall boom on a tripod was positioned next to the stack. The loader on a hayrack would plunge a hayfork into the load. My job was to drive the horse team that moved the steel cable through a pulley, tipping the boom arm, drawing the hay up. When it reached the pulley, the loader would swing it over the stack and, when properly positioned, jerk the trip. The hay cascaded onto the top of the stack. A man on the stack spread it evenly (otherwise the hay would slide off). It was a source of pride to produce a tall, well-rounded stack.

One day, lightning struck the tripod and traveled from the boom through the cable, knocking me senseless. This was probably a good thing, because the horses tried to bolt. The whole contraption came down—which kept the horses from getting far—but I had to be untangled from the equipment.

I was mangled pretty badly. Mr. Baldwin paid the hospital bill, but my arm and hand were never the same after that. I didn't let it stop me. The next summer I was back on the job. By holding one rein in the crook of my arm, I could ease the strain that simple grasping put on my poor hand as the day wore on.

Mr. Baldwin owned the finest pair of Percheron draft horses I'd ever seen. They must have weighed about 1,400 pounds apiece. Charlie Scott, from up the valley, had been hired to drive this big team. He was a strapping fellow (he must have weighed over 200 pounds) inclined to be somewhat of a braggart. Only about four years my senior, he let me know often that I was just a kid.

An old wagon chassis had been converted into a cook wagon. On the noon break it would be nearby to feed the crew. We had an hour for lunch because the teams required that much time to consume the hay and oats they needed.

Charlie claimed "his" team could out-pull and out-work any team on the spread. Waving his nose at Son and Tad, he said "A good, stiff wind would blow them jackrabbits sideways."

Something like this went on nearly every time we nooned. I guess my dad got a little tired of the continual ribbing. One day he said, "Tell you what, Charlie. There's a hundred-acre field of hay mowed four days ago. I'll bet you a week's pay that my team of 'jackrabbits' will rake half of it before your team can."

"You gotta be kiddin'," said Chalie. "Those scrawny ewes would barely be starting by the time I finished. Tell you what: I'll give you two weeks' pay if your time is better than mine. Since yours is the slowest team, I'll lead off and let them eat my dust."

"How about passing?"

"That's a laugh—you can't pass what you can't catch! Pass anytime you get the chance."

"Inside?"

"Why not? You'll never get close enough."

The race was set for Saturday.

After work I walked Son and Tad toward the corral to brush them down. Sam Cole, the Negro cook, was watching Mr.

Baldwin's prize stud cavorting around the field. It was a picture as the horse crow-hopped and kicked up his heels in sheer jubilation at being alive. As he ran around the pasture with his mane and tail fluttering in the wind, Sam said, "Man-o-man, that black beauty is plumb full o' proud!" I agreed, but my eye was taken by something even more impressive in the corral—a thing of enchantment.

She was a sorrel filly with mane and tail of pure palomino gold. Her large, lambent eyes were separated by a white blaze. Her dainty, white-stockinged legs seemed to let her float over the ground, almost angel-like. I figured if a cat could look at a king, it would be alright if I looked at a queen. To me, she was more than royalty—I was in love. But I had to take care of my team.

The next day I showed up early for a proper introduction. Ginger was as sweet as she was pretty. After getting permission from Mr. Baldwin, I approached her, humming softly. Soon we were riding around the corral. She was so smooth—she's the only horse I trusted with the reins in my bad hand alone.

When Saturday came, my Dad said, "Dave, you're drivin' the team."

"Me? You've had more experience."

"You can handle it."

Dad could see my insecurity. "Have you ever had a reason to doubt my judgment?"

"No sir."

"Listen. You know this team—and you've run the rake plenty—so I don't have to tell you how to do that. If you don't kick the trip at the right time, don't worry; you're not trying to win a prize for the straightest rows."

Charlie was positioned ahead of me. Dad whispered "Hold old Son and Tad back a little. Don't give them their heads until I wave my hat." I wrapped one of the lines around my bad arm and, at the signal, we were out.

In the first round, Charlie led by several lengths. When three quarters of the field had been raked, Charlie was nearly an entire lap ahead of me. The turns were getting tighter as we moved closer to the middle of the field.

Both my arms ached from the strain of holding my team back, but my bum arm began to throb. I figured we had about six laps to go when I saw my dad swing his hat back and forth. I let up on the lines, and that team swung into a perfectly synchronized reaching gait that began eating up the distance between me and the Percherons. About three more laps would see the job done. Now my leg was giving me pain from the continual kicking of the trip lever. By this time, I was right behind Charlie's team. Sweat darkened Son and Tad's coats. But Charlie's team was fighting for breath, sides heaving. Charlie gave one agonized look over his shoulder and began beating his team with the ends of his lines.

On the last lap, I cut inside Charlie's path. The crew was shouting. The wheels of the rake tore up clods and dust as they spun along. Coming down the last stretch we were almost neck and neck. Now I was oblivious to my arms and leg. I could see the post that marked the finish. It seemed to approach with maddening slowness.

I was afraid to take a good look at the draft team so close beside me. By this time, they had broken into a lumbering gallop as Charlie flayed their rumps with the lines. Even so, their position didn't seem to change. I urged my team with a pleading voice and shook the lines over their straining backs. Their bellies got closer to the ground as those long legs moved with the smoothness of pistons that belied the contraption behind them. They knew they were in a race, and they seemed eager to get their noses under the wire first. Their necks reached out and their manes flew back from the wind of their motion.

We reached the finish about three lengths ahead of Charlie's team. The whole crew was dancing up and down, whooping and yelling like Comanches. Old Son and Tad were still pulling at the bits as I stiffly got off the rig. About this time Charlie's rig pulled up. He jumped from the seat and rushed at me. He gave me a shove that put me on my back and knocked the wind out of me. "You cheated on the turn! You cheated on the turn!" he yelled.

Mr. Baldwin and Dad grabbed Charlie by each arm. I got up slowly just as Mr. Baldwin said, "You're through here, Charlie. You damn-near foundered a good team! Go to the cook shack and get your time."

This wasn't a large High Sierra valley. Most everyone knew a little about everyone else. I knew Charlie had been orphaned when he was twelve and that a crotchety uncle had assumed the unwanted job of raising him. I also knew that once you were fired by Mr. Baldwin, hardly any rancher in the valley would have you on his place. I saw crestfallen, embarrassed panic in Charlie's eyes. "Mr. Baldwin," I said, "don't fire Charlie. He might have won if I hadn't been fifty pounds lighter. It might not have been fair."

Charlie stood between the two men looking desperate and ashamed. It wasn't about a lost race or two week's wages anymore; he knew in his heart he'd been a poor loser and used his size to push someone smaller than he.

Mr. Baldwin stared at me real hard, as though a little affronted at a kid butting into what should be a man's affair. After a moment he said to Charlie, "Get your butt over to that team and take their harnesses off. I don't have to tell you how to cool them down. That pair cost me a thousand dollars; if I find they're ruined I'll take it out of your future wages!"

Then he laid a big hand on my shoulder. With a sort of affection in his eye, he said, "David, I've seen you with that little quarter-horse filly in the corral. You taking a shine to that little mare?" Well, I didn't know what to say. "Since you've shown you've learned a little of what it takes to be a man today, I'd feel very proud if you'd accept Ginger as a gift from me."

Here I was, just a kid, and the most important man in the valley was paying me an honor. Not only that, he actually asked me to accept something that I'd never hoped to own in my wildest dreams. My throat was so tightened up I couldn't get a word of appreciation out. I felt like a blockhead, just standing there.

Dad and Mr. Baldwin were looking at me with smiles on their faces. I looked over at the crew. They were all grinning and laughing. I knew they weren't laughing at me, just sharing the joy that infused my face. I turned tail and ran like a scared rabbit in the direction of the corral, where my new love waited with that proud neck arched. Her soft muzzle pushed toward me to be petted.

When Charlie finished his summer work for Mr. Baldwin, he came to work for us at Dad's invitation. He'd lost his cocky ways and we hunted and fished together. Also, I think he was kinda stuck on Julia, my sister.

Today I was turning sixteen, heading into the barn to see my Ginger. But where was she? My heart thundered—could she have been stolen? My fear turned to dismay when I found her standing in the sun by the ten-foot-wide doors. I stopped. She was decked out like I'd never seen her before.

As I approached, I could hardly believe the sight. There was a brand-spanking-new saddle on her back. I knew it was a Visalia hull—the best. And how she set it off! She had perfect conformation and seemed proud to be wearing it. A little sign said, "From Mom and Dad."

Hanging from the saddle horn was a fine pair of Justin boots. The note said "Love, Julia." Those stinkers in the house hadn't said a word this morning—hardly gave me the time of day. My cup of ecstasy was about as full as it could get, or so I thought.

But, I had yet to experience the biggest thrill of all—the

most, the greatest—a thrill that shook me down to my old, scruffy boots! Between the new Navajo saddle-blanket and the saddle skirt was an envelope. I pulled it out and tore it open. Boy-o-boy, that dirty, rotten, sneaking coyote Charlie Scott had stolen my Ginger out of the barn—behind my back! He and my folks had connived with that low-life, Bill Baldwin, to breed my Ginger to that big black stud. Ginger's foal would be fully pedigreed with a noble lineage going back six generations and registered in the stud book.

My semi-shocked condition must have been an entertaining scene. From the corner of my eye, I noticed Mom, Dad, Julia, and Charlie with smiles that nearly split their faces. "Happy Birthday!" they said.

Man, as old Sam might have observed, that sunlit barn was surely "full o' proud!" Ginger turned her head and nudged my bum elbow with her velvety nose. She didn't care about pedigrees; she was just happy to see me!

About the Authors

Ransom "Doc" Wilcox was born in Taber, Alberta, Canada, in 1907 to David Adrian and Agnes Southworth Wilcox. He was the sixth of seven children. Because Rance was sickly, it was suggested that the family move to California. The family was part of a group of Latter-day Saints (Mormons) that bought land in Vina, north of Chico in 1907. Financial hardship forced the family to move often in search of work: Vacaville, Pope Valley, Gridley, Ukiah, Redwood Valley, Sebastopol, and Oakland.

They farmed and tended livestock: sheep, cattle, horses, pigs, turkeys, and hens. They cured ham in a smoke house and did a lot of hunting and fishing in the Sierra Nevada Mountains. Once, to escape a charging boar, Wilcox stuck a pole he was carrying in the ground and climbed up!

One season the family lived in a tent while the men worked cutting hay. At harvest time everyone picked apples. Another year, Wilcox joined his father and brothers in Arizona, building a school on an American Indian reservation. Many elements of Wilcox's stories come from his early experiences (though it was his younger brother who was crippled—by polio—and there was no gift of a mare).

In 1935 Wilcox married and began studying to be a chiropractor. But the Great Depression put his studies on hold. He tried several enterprises to support his family—most failed. So did the marriage.

In 1943 he enlisted in the army. Because of his hunting background they had him train soldiers in gunnery and target practice. Just before his unit was to go overseas, Wilcox got the flu. He missed the boat—literally—so was honorably discharged.

Between more failed marriages, Wilcox completed his studies and opened a chiropractic practice just off Union Square in San Francisco. He took his kids to see Coit Tower, Fisherman's Wharf, Seal Rock, Smugglers' Cove, the Presidio, Fleishhacker Zoo, and football games at Kezar Stadium. Later he moved to Hayward and opened a practice on B Street.

His friends called him Ray (for R.A.) or Doc. Besides writing, Wilcox was an excellent dancer. He enjoyed singing and was good with his hands. He loved to walk in the great outdoors. Near the end of his life, he joked about leaving his body to science; "I'm sure they can use my brain. It's in perfect condition—never been used." In a letter to his daughter, he wrote "In my heart I have no hatred or dislike for anyone. In my career I have eased many a person's pain and suffering." Wilcox died of cancer in 1992 and is buried in Ukiah, CA. His short stories and poems are published under the title, *Horse & Dog Adventures in Early California.*

Karl Beckstrand is the author of fourteen books and more than 40 online titles (reviews by Kirkus, The Horn Book blog, *School Library Journal, ForeWord Reviews*). Raised in San Jose, California, USA, he received a B.A. in journalism from BYU and an M.A. in international relations from APU. Two publishers produced his early titles. In 2004 he founded Premio Publishing & Gozo Books.

Beckstrand inherited *To Swallow the Earth* as an incomplete manuscript and carefully honed the characters while preserving the original story's action and earthy vernacular. He teaches mass media at a state university and speaks on traditional vs. digital/self-publishing.

Beckstrand has lived abroad, been a Spanish/English interpreter, and enjoys volleyball and kayaking (usually not at the same time). His nonfiction/biographies, fiction, Spanish & bilingual books, e-book mysteries, and app feature diverse characters and usually end with a twist. His multicultural work has appeared in: Barnes & Noble, Border's Books, Deseret Book, Costco, Kindle/Amazon, Sony, Kobo, iBooks, The Children's Miracle Network, *The Congressional Record* of the U.S. House of Representatives, *Papercrafts Magazine,* LDS Film Festival, and various broadcasts. Find: "Karl Beckstrand – Author" on FB, Amazon, Twitter, and KarlBeckstrand.com.